Lost at the School Swimming Pool – Mystery of the Missing Kids

HAMZA ANSARI

TABLE OF CONTENT

1
A Journey of Friendship

The alarm clock buzzed loudly, signaling the start of a new school year. Levi groaned and pulled the covers over his head. "Levi, it's time to get up!" his mother called from the kitchen.

Levi sighed and dragged himself out of bed. He quickly got dressed and grabbed his backpack. As he entered the kitchen, his mother handed him a piece of toast. "Nervous about the first day?" she asked.

"A little," he admitted. "But I'm excited to see Ramy and Kellie."

His mother smiled. "You'll do great, Levi. Just be yourself."

Levi nodded, feeling a bit more confident. He hurried out the door, walking with his distinctive, slightly uneven gait. The familiar streets buzzed with the energy of other kids heading to their first day.

Levi's steps were measured and careful, his right leg moving with a slight limp, a reminder of the injury he had sustained when he was younger. He had learned to live with it, but it still made him self-conscious.

As Levi approached the school, he could feel the stares of some of the other kids. They didn't mean any harm, but their curious looks always made him feel a little different. He took a deep breath and focused on the sight of his friends waiting for him by the entrance.

Levi smiled and made his way to Ramy, who immediately started cracking jokes. "Why did the math book look sad? Because it had too many problems!"

Levi chuckled. "Same old Ramy."

Kellie was already seated next to them, her supplies neatly arranged. Kellie was two years older than Levi and Ramy. Her parents had lived in a remote village where there was no school, so she started her education later than most kids. Her mother had passed away when she was very young, and her father had moved to town to ensure Kellie could attend school and support her studies.

Despite the challenges, Kellie was strong and determined, often acting as a big sister to her friends. "You two better not get us into trouble this year," she warned.

Ramy grinned. "Trouble? Us? Never."

The teacher, Mrs. Thompson, called the class to order. "Welcome back, everyone. I hope you all had a wonderful summer. Let's get started with some introductions."

The students took turns introducing themselves, sharing a bit about their summer vacations. When it was Levi's turn, he stood up nervously. "Hi, I'm Levi. I spent most of my summer helping my mom at the bookshop."

Freddy snickered from the other side of the room. "What a nerd."

Kellie shot Freddy a glare. "At least Levi's doing something useful."

Freddy rolled his eyes and muttered something under his breath.

The bell rang for lunch, and the students poured out of the classroom. Levi, Ramy, and Kellie headed to their usual spot under the big oak tree in the schoolyard.

Ramy pulled out a bag of chips. "So, did you guys hear about Mr. Thompson's new rule? No chewing gum in class."

Levi laughed. "Good luck enforcing that."

Kellie shook her head. "Especially with you, Ramy. You're always chewing something."

Ramy grinned. "What can I say? I'm a rebel."

Their laughter was interrupted by Lilly and Freddy approaching them. "Look who it is," Lilly sneered. "The nerd squads."

Kellie stood up. "Leave us alone, Lilly."

Freddy crossed his arms. "Or what?"

Ramy, always the peacemaker, tried to lighten the mood. "Hey, Freddy, did you hear the one about the pencil? It had a point, but it was really dull."

Lilly rolled her eyes. "You guys are pathetic."

Levi clenched his fists but stayed silent. He didn't want to give them the satisfaction of seeing him upset.

As the day went on, Levi couldn't shake off the comments from Lilly and Freddy. During recess, he sat alone on a bench, lost in thought. Kellie noticed and walked over to him. "Hey, you, okay?"

Levi sighed. "I just hate how they always make fun of me. It's like I can't do anything right."

Kellie put a comforting hand on his shoulder. "Don't listen to them, Levi. They're just jealous because you're kind and smart."

Levi looked up at her, his eyes filled with uncertainty. "You really think so?"

"Absolutely," Kellie said firmly. "And Ramy and I are here for you, no matter what."

Just then, Ramy bounded over, out of breath from running. "Hey, Levi! You won't believe what I just saw! A squirrel stole a kid's sandwich!"

Levi couldn't help but laugh at Ramy's excitement.

During lunch, Levi, Ramy, and Kellie settled under the big oak tree. A few minutes later, two older students approached them. "Hey, Kellie!" Brittany waved, her blonde hair catching the sunlight. Brittany was known for her sharp wit and infectious laugh.

"Hi, Brittany! Andrew, how's it going?" Kellie greeted them warmly. Andrew, tall and always carrying a book, was the science whiz of their grade.

Andrew smiled. "Good, just gearing up for the science fair. You should join us in the library later."

Kellie nodded. "Sounds fun. I'll catch up with you guys after school."

Ramy couldn't resist. "Careful, Kellie. Spend too much time with those nerds, and you'll start quoting Shakespeare and talking about quantum physics."

Brittany laughed. "Better that than spending time with a class clown who thinks 'pi' is just something you eat."

Levi chuckled while Ramy feigned offense. "Hey, I happen to like pie. And I'm pretty sure Einstein did too."

Kellie giggled. "Come on, guys. Be nice."

Andrew rolled his eyes but smiled slightly. "Yeah, yeah. Just don't expect to see Ramy at the science fair unless there's free food involved."

Ramy grinned. "As long as there's pie, I'm there."

Brittany smirked. "Maybe we should have a pie-eating contest instead of a science fair."

Kellie laughed, but Andrew's face turned serious. "Very funny, Ramy. At least we're doing something productive. Unlike hanging out with—" Andrew paused, glancing at Levi, "certain people."

Levi's smile faded, and Ramy's eyes narrowed. "What's that supposed to mean?"

Andrew shrugged. "Nothing, just that maybe Kellie could spend her time more wisely than hanging out with—"

Kellie cut in; her voice sharp. "Andrew, don't you dare. Levi is my friend, and he's worth more than your entire science project."

Brittany looked uncomfortable. "Hey, let's not fight, guys."

Andrew felt a pang of guilt but continued, "I'm just saying, hanging out with someone who—"

"Someone who what?" Kellie snapped. "Someone who's different? Levi's a better person than you'll ever be if you keep talking like that."

Andrew realized he had crossed a line. He glanced at Levi, who looked hurt, and at Ramy, whose fists were clenched.

"Levi, I'm sorry. I didn't mean it that way," Andrew said quietly. "I was just... I don't know. Trying to be funny. It wasn't right."

Levi nodded slowly, still hurt but willing to listen. "Okay, Andrew. Just... be careful with your words."

Ramy chimed in, his tone still angry. "Yeah, next time think before you speak."

Andrew nodded, feeling the weight of his mistake. "I'm really sorry, guys. Can we start over?"

Kellie's expression softened. "Just remember, Andrew, respect matters."

Brittany, trying to lighten the mood, said, "So, how about we all head to the canteen? I could use a drink."

Everyone agreed, the tension easing as they walked together towards the canteen. Andrew fell in step beside Levi. "Really, Levi, I'm sorry. Friends?"

Levi offered a small smile. "Friends."

They reached the canteen, grabbed a few drinks, and found a table. The group sat down, the earlier conflict giving way to light-hearted conversation and laughter as they enjoyed each other's company.

After school, the trio of Kellie, Levi and ramy decided to stop by the local ice cream shop. They were enjoying their treats when Lilly and Freddy walked in.

"Great, just what we needed," Kellie muttered.

Lilly sauntered over, a smirk on her face. "What's up, losers? Enjoying your ice cream?"

Ramy, "Yep! Want some? Oh wait, I forgot. You're already full of it."

Freddy stepped forward, anger flashing in his eyes. "What did you say?"

Levi stepped between them, trying to avoid a confrontation. "Come on, guys. Let's just enjoy our ice cream."

Freddy shoved Levi, causing him to stumble. "Stay out of this, limp boy."

Ramy's face turned serious. "Hey! That's enough. Don't you dare touch him."

Kellie moved closer, ready to defend her friends. "You need to leave. Now."

Lilly and Freddy glared at them before turning to leave. "This isn't over," Freddy warned.

Kellie sighed. "Let's just get out of here."

The next day, the students were buzzing with excitement about the start of swimming pool classes. Levi, Ramy, and Kellie gathered in the locker room, changing into their swimsuits.

Ramy, ever the jokester, pulled on his goggles and struck a pose. "Check me out, guys. Future Olympic swimmer right here!"

Kellie laughed. "You look ridiculous, Ramy."

Levi adjusted his swim trunks nervously. "I'm not sure about this. What if I can't do it?"

Kellie placed a reassuring hand on his shoulder. "You'll be fine, Levi. We're all in this together."

Ramy nodded. "Yeah, and if you drown, I'll give you mouth-to-mouth."

Levi chuckled. "Thanks, Ramy. That's very reassuring."

The students gathered around the pool, their instructor, Coach Harper, greeting them with a warm smile. "Alright, everyone. Today we're starting with the basics. Floating and kicking. Let's see what you've got."

The class was divided into small groups. Levi, Ramy, and Kellie were in the same group, while Lilly and Freddy were in another.

Ramy tried to lighten the mood. "Just think of it as a big bathtub!"

Levi gave a nervous laugh. "Sure, if bathtubs were this huge."

Coach Harper demonstrated the floating technique, and the students followed suit. Levi struggled at first, his movements awkward and unsure.

From across the pool, Freddy shouted, "Hey look! Levi's trying to swim like a duck!"

Lilly added, "More like a sinking rock!"

Kellie shot back, "Ignore them, Levi. You're doing great."

Ramy, ever the peacemaker, chimed in with a joke. "Freddy, let's see you try not to sink with all that hot air."

Freddy glared, but Levi felt a surge of confidence from his friends' support.

After the swim class, Levi sat by the pool, feeling disheartened. Kellie joined him, handing him a towel. "Hey, don't let them get to you."

Levi sighed. "It's just... I want to be good at something. Anything."

Kellie gave him a reassuring smile. "You are good at things, Levi. You're smart, kind, and brave. Swimming is just another thing you'll conquer."

Ramy plopped down next to them, dripping wet. "And hey, even if we don't win any medals, at least we'll have some funny stories to tell."

Levi chuckled.

The next day, the swim class continued, and Levi was determined to improve. However, Freddy and Lilly's taunts didn't stop. As they practiced swimming across the pool, Freddy splashed water at Levi, causing him to lose focus and struggle.

Lilly laughed. "Look at him flailing around!"

Kellie was quick to defend him. "Leave him alone, Lilly!"

Freddy smirked. "Or what?"

Ramy stepped in. "Or you'll have to deal with both of us."

Freddy rolled his eyes but backed off, muttering under his breath.

Coach Harper noticed the commotion. "Is there a problem here?"

Levi shook his head. "No, Coach. We're fine."

Coach Harper nodded but kept a close eye on the group.

By the end of the week, Levi was starting to get the hang of swimming. He still had a long way to go, but he felt more confident with each practice.

One day, after a particularly good session, Ramy pulled Levi aside. "Hey, Levi. You're really improving. I bet you'll be swimming laps around Freddy in no time."

Levi smiled. "Thanks, Ramy.

Kellie joined them, beaming. "We're a team, Levi. And together, we can do anything."

Ramy struck another silly pose. "And remember, if you ever need a lifeguard, I'm your guy!"

Levi laughed. "I'll keep that in mind."

The final swim class of the week had everyone on edge. Coach Harper announced, "Today, we'll be having a short race to see how far you've come. Remember, this is just for fun."

Levi felt a mix of excitement and nerves. "I can do this," he whispered to himself.

As the race began, Levi focused on everything he had practiced. However, halfway through, he felt a sharp pain in his right leg. His pace slowed, and he struggled to keep up. Freddy noticed and took advantage, splashing water directly at Levi's face.

"What's the matter, Levi? Can't keep up?" Freddy taunted.

Lilly added, "Maybe swimming isn't your thing. Maybe nothing is."

Levi's confidence shattered. He coughed and sputtered, trying to regain his rhythm, but the pain and the taunts overwhelmed him. He barely made it to the end of the pool, feeling utterly defeated.

Ramy and Kellie rushed to his side. "Levi, are you okay?" Kellie asked, concern etched on her face.

Levi shook his head, tears mixing with the pool water. "I failed. I couldn't do it."

Ramy tried to cheer him up. "Come on, Levi. You did your best. That's what matters."

But Levi couldn't shake off the feeling of failure. "No, Ramy. I didn't just fail. I embarrassed myself."

Freddy and Lilly's laughter echoed in the background. "Nice try, Levi! Better luck next time," Freddy sneered.

Levi felt a wave of sadness and humiliation wash over him. Despite Ramy and Kellie's support, he couldn't calm down. The mocking laughter and the stares of his classmates made him feel isolated and alone.

That night, Levi lay in bed, staring at the ceiling. He replayed the day's events over and over in his mind. His mother's soft knock on the door brought him back to reality.

"Levi, honey, are you okay?" she asked gently.

Levi shook his head, unable to speak. His mother sat beside him, stroking his hair. "It's okay to have bad days, Levi. It's part of life."

"But why does it have to be so hard?" he whispered.

She sighed, her heart aching for her son. "Because sometimes, the hardest moments are the ones that make us stronger."

Levi turned away, tears streaming down his face. "I just want to be good at something. I want to stop feeling like a failure."

His mother hugged him tightly. "You are good at many things, Levi. And you have the biggest heart of anyone I know."

The next day at school, Levi avoided the pool and his friends. He didn't want their pity or their encouragement. He just wanted to be alone. During lunch, he sat under the oak tree, the one place that used to bring him comfort. But today, it felt different.

The laughter and chatter of other kids seemed distant, and he felt a deep sense of loneliness.

Kellie found him there, sitting with his head down. She approached cautiously. "Levi, can we talk?"

Levi didn't look up. "I don't want to talk, Kellie. I just want to be alone."

Kellie sat beside him; her voice soft. "We just want to help."

Levi finally looked at her, his eyes red from crying. "I know. But right now, nothing you say will make me feel better."

Ramy joined them, sitting on the other side of Levi. "We get it, man. Just know we're here when you're ready."

Levi nodded, appreciating their presence even if he couldn't fully embrace it yet.

As the days passed, Levi struggled to find his usual spark. The weight of failure and the constant teasing from Freddy and Lilly hung over him like a dark cloud. Despite his friends' best efforts, the sense of loneliness and sadness lingered.

One afternoon, Kellie decided to confront Freddy and Lilly. "You guys need to stop. You don't understand what you're doing to Levi."

Freddy shrugged. "It's just some fun. He needs to toughen up."

Kellie's eyes blazed with anger. "It's not fun. It's cruel. And it's hurting him."

Lilly rolled her eyes. "Why do you care so much?"

"Because he's, my friend" Kellie said firmly.

Freddy and Lilly seemed unmoved, but Kellie hoped her words would at least make them think.

Back at home, Levi's mother noticed his ongoing struggle. "Levi, I know things have been tough. But remember, it's okay to ask for help."

Levi nodded slowly. "I just feel so lost, Mom."

She hugged him again. "It's okay to feel lost. But don't forget, you have people who care about you."

Levi sighed, knowing she was right but still feeling the weight of his emotions.

The next day, Levi went to school, feeling the heavy weight of his sadness. As he walked into the classroom, Kellie and Ramy immediately noticed his demeanor.

"Levi, you, okay?" Kellie asked gently, her eyes filled with concern.

Ramy tried to lighten the mood. "Hey buddy, why did the scarecrow win an award? Because he was outstanding in his field!"

Levi forced a small smile but didn't respond. He quietly took his seat, his mind elsewhere.

During lunch, they all sat under the oak tree, but the usual laughter and chatter were absent. Ramy tried again. "Levi, did you hear about the mathematician who's afraid of negative numbers? He'll stop at nothing to avoid them!"

Despite the effort, Levi remained unresponsive, lost in his thoughts. Kellie sighed, feeling awkward and disappointed. "Maybe he just needs some space," she whispered to Ramy.

Over the next few days, Kellie and Ramy kept their distance, unsure of how to help their friend. The absence of their company made Levi feel even more isolated. He sat alone at lunch, watching as his friends interacted with others, their laughter seeming to mock his loneliness.

One afternoon, Levi decided to approach Kellie and Ramy, hoping to mend their friendship. He found them by the lockers, talking and laughing with a few classmates.

"Hey, guys," Levi said hesitantly.

Kellie glanced at him, her smile fading. "Oh, hey, Levi."

Ramy gave a half-hearted nod. "Hey."

Levi's heart sank. "I... I just wanted to say I'm sorry. For pushing you guys away."

Kellie looked away; her expression unreadable. "It's okay, Levi. We get it."

Feeling more alone than ever, Levi turned and walked away, tears stinging his eyes. He spent the rest of the day avoiding everyone, retreating into his shell.

Later that evening, as Ramy and Kellie were walking home together, they talked about Levi.

"Do you think we were too hard on him?" Ramy asked, guilt evident in his voice.

Kellie sighed. "Maybe. I just didn't know how to help him. And seeing him so sad... it hurt."

"We can't just leave him like this," Ramy said firmly. "He needs us."

Kellie nodded. "You're right. Tomorrow, we make things right."

The next day, Kellie and Ramy sought out Levi during lunch. They found him sitting alone under the oak tree, his head down.

"Hey, Levi," Kellie said softly.

Levi looked up, surprised to see them. "Hi."

Ramy sat down next to him. "We've missed you, man. And we're sorry for not being there when you needed us."

Kellie sat on Levi's other side, her eyes welling up. "We just want to help, Levi. We didn't mean to make you feel worse."

Levi's voice trembled. "I felt so alone. Like I couldn't do anything right."

Ramy put an arm around Levi's shoulders. "You don't have to do everything right. We're here for you, no matter what."

Kellie wiped away a tear, smiling through her emotions. "Can you forgive us for being distant?"

Levi nodded, tears streaming down his face. "I'm sorry, too. I shouldn't have pushed you away."

They all sat there in silence for a moment, the bond of their friendship stronger than ever. Then Ramy, true to form, broke the tension with a joke. "Okay, now that the mushy stuff is over, why don't we get back to something important? Like figuring out who put glue on Mr. Thompson's chair!"

Levi laughed, a genuine laugh that felt like a release. "That sounds like something you would do, Ramy."

Kellie chuckled. "Yeah, it definitely does."

Ramy grinned. "Guilty as charged. But hey, it got us to laugh, right?"

Levi smiled, feeling a sense of warmth and belonging. "Thanks, guys. I really needed this."

Kellie hugged him. "We're a team, Levi. And we always will be."

Ramy, unable to resist, added one last joke. "And remember, if you ever need a lifeguard, I'm your guy!"

They all laughed, the sound carrying across the schoolyard, a testament to the strength of their friendship and the resilience of their spirits.

2

Levi's Underwater Discovery

Since Levi hadn't been to swimming class for a while, Kellie was determined to get him back in the water. "Come on, Levi, you can't let one bad experience keep you from trying again," she insisted.

Levi sighed. "I know, Kellie. It's just hard to get back into it."

Kellie nodded sympathetically. "I get it. But you're stronger than you think. Let's just go and have fun, no pressure."

Ramy chimed in with his usual humor. "Yeah, Levi. Plus, who else is going to help me win the 'slowest swimmer' award?"

Levi chuckled. "Alright, you win. Let's do this."

On the day of the swimming class, the trio suited up and headed to the pool. The atmosphere was electric, with the upcoming swimming competition adding a sense of urgency to their training.

Coach Harper gathered the students. "Alright, everyone. Today, we're pushing our limits. I want to see your best efforts."

Kellie gave Levi an encouraging nod. "You've got this."

As the training began, Levi felt a surge of determination. He swam with more strength and confidence than ever before. But as he pushed himself harder, he inadvertently crossed into the deeper, adult side of the pool.

"Levi, slow down!" Kellie called out, but Levi was too focused to hear.

Levi felt the water growing colder and the pressure increasing as he ventured deeper. Suddenly, he lost control and started to sink. Panic set in, but he forced himself to stay calm and look around. At the bottom of the pool, something strange caught his eye.

He saw what looked like an old, rusted lever. Driven by curiosity, Levi swam closer and pressed it. The floor beneath him shifted, and to his shock, a hidden door opened, sucking him inside before he could react.

Levi tumbled through a dark tunnel, finally landing in a large, dry room. He stood up, disoriented and gasping for breath. As his eyes adjusted to the dim light, he saw something that made his jaw drop.

The underground facility was massive, resembling a factory. Conveyor belts, machinery, and strange, glowing panels filled the space. Levi spotted a ladder against the wall, which seemed to be the only way out.

Levi's heart pounded as he cautiously approached the ladder. He climbed down, his mind racing with questions. How could such a place exist beneath the swimming pool? And what was its purpose?

As he descended, he noticed the facility was eerily silent. He walked around, trying to make sense of the bizarre environment. He saw machines that appeared to be powered by an unknown energy source, and storage tanks filled with mysterious substances.

Levi's mind buzzed with theories. Was this some kind of secret lab? A hidden government facility? The possibilities seemed endless and frightening.

Back at the pool, the swimming class continued without any idea of Levi's disappearance. The students were too focused on their training for the upcoming competition, and Coach Harper was busy supervising them.

Kellie and Ramy, initially worried when they lost sight of Levi, assumed he was taking a break or practicing elsewhere in the pool. "He'll be fine," Kellie reassured herself, though she couldn't shake off a nagging feeling of concern.

Meanwhile, Levi explored deeper into the facility, looking for a way out. He stumbled upon a control room filled with screens and buttons. He pressed a few, hoping to find an exit, but the screens only displayed confusing data and schematics.

He found a door marked "Exit" but it was locked tight. Desperation set in as he realized he was trapped. He banged on the door, hoping someone above might hear him, but the sound barely echoed in the vast, empty space.

Levi slumped to the floor, feeling the weight of his situation. "How am I going to get out of here?" he muttered to himself. Just then, he noticed a small ventilation shaft above him. It was a tight squeeze, but it seemed to be his only option.

He climbed up and wriggled through the shaft, his heart pounding with each movement. After what felt like an eternity, he saw a faint light at the end. Summoning all his strength, Levi pushed forward and finally emerged into a small maintenance room.

As Levi entered the maintenance room, his eyes immediately fell on a row of CCTV screens. Each one displayed different areas of the vast underground facility. He saw various labs, bustling with activity, where people in lab coats worked on strange experiments.

A sense of dread washed over him as he realized the magnitude of what he had stumbled upon. He checked the control panel and was relieved to find that there were no cameras in the maintenance room itself. "At least they can't see me here," he thought.

Levi cautiously approached the screens, his heart pounding. He saw scientists conducting experiments on animals and strange machines emitting eerie glows. But what caught his attention the most was a series of screens showing rooms filled with children, around his age or younger, all locked up.

The children looked scared and confused, some huddled together, others sitting alone, staring blankly at the walls. Levi's stomach churned. "Who are these kids? What are they doing here?"

One screen showed a large room labeled "Test Subjects: 50-100," and another screen labeled "Isolation." The realization hit him hard—these were missing children, taken from their homes, their lives.

As Levi continued to watch, he overheard snippets of conversation from a nearby intercom. "Subjects 32 through 45 are ready for phase three," a voice said. "Ensure all medical equipment is prepared for the transfer."

Levi's heart raced. They were planning to use these children for medical experiments. The thought was horrifying. He saw kids being led into rooms with strange machines, hooked up to monitors and IVs. Some were crying, others looked too exhausted to react.

He quickly grabbed a notepad and began jotting down everything he saw and heard. The faces of the children were etched into his memory, and he vowed to do something to help them.

Levi knew he couldn't stay hidden forever. He needed to find a way out and get help. He scanned the room for any useful information. A map of the facility caught his eye. It showed various exits and security checkpoints. He traced his route back to the swimming pool but realized it was heavily guarded.

He noticed a ventilation shaft that seemed to lead towards an older, less guarded part of the facility. "That's my way out," he decided. But first, he needed more evidence.

Levi searched the room for anything he could use to prove what he had seen. He found a stack of files labeled "Subject Reports" and began skimming through them. Each report detailed the abduction and subsequent experiments on children from different countries. It was chilling to read about the cold, clinical way the scientists described their subjects.

He looked around for something to protect the documents from getting wet when he returned to the pool. He found a plastic cover and carefully placed the most critical documents inside, sealing them tightly.

As he continued to explore the room, he found a hidden drawer with more disturbing documents. They detailed plans for future experiments, including genetic modifications and dangerous drug trials. The goal was clear: these scientists were trying to create some form of enhanced humans, using the children as unwilling subjects.

Levi felt a surge of anger. "How could anyone do this?" he whispered to himself. He knew he had to get out of there and expose this nightmare. He added these documents to the plastic-covered pile, ensuring they were secure.

As Levi continued to explore the room, he found a hidden drawer with more disturbing documents. They detailed plans for future experiments, including genetic modifications and dangerous drug trials. The goal was clear: these scientists were trying to create some form of enhanced humans, using the children as unwilling subjects.

Levi felt a surge of anger. "How could anyone do this?" he whispered to himself. He knew he had to get out of there and expose this nightmare. He quickly added these documents to the plastic-covered pile, ensuring they were secure.

Levi carefully climbed into the ventilation shaft, making sure to stay quiet. The narrow space was dark and cramped, but he pressed on, guided by the map he had memorized. After what felt like an eternity, he reached an old storage room.

He pushed open the grate and slipped out, finding himself in a dusty, forgotten part of the facility. He cautiously made his way to an exit door marked on the map. To his relief, it wasn't locked.

Clutching the plastic-covered documents, Levi knew he had to get back to the pool without raising suspicion. He emerged into the pool area, still holding his breath. The plastic cover kept the documents dry, much to his relief.

However, as he hurried towards the exit, he heard footsteps and voices approaching the maintenance room. Panicking, he dropped the documents in his rush to escape. He couldn't go back for them now; his only choice was to get out and get help.

Levi quickly made his way back to the edge of the pool where the swim class was finishing up. The sight of his friends training brought a wave of relief.

"Levi! There you are!" Kellie exclaimed, rushing to him.

Ramy looked equally concerned. "We've been looking everywhere for you!"

Levi surfaced from the pool, gasping for breath. Kellie rushed over to him, her face a mix of relief and worry. "Levi! Where have you been? We were so worried!"

Levi was still in shock, his mind racing with everything he had seen. "Kellie, I... I need to tell you something. It's important."

Once the swim class finished, Levi, Kellie, and Ramy gathered their things. "Meet me at our usual spot," Levi said, his voice trembling. "I need to explain something."

Curious and concerned, Kellie and Ramy followed Levi to their favorite spot under the oak tree. They sat down, and Levi took a deep breath.

"I found something," Levi began, his voice shaking. "There's an underground facility beneath the pool. It's huge, like a factory.

And there are kids—lots of them—being held there. They're planning to use them for medical experiments."

Kellie and Ramy exchanged skeptical glances. "Levi, are you serious?" Kellie asked, trying to understand.

Ramy laughed nervously. "This sounds like something out of a movie, Levi. Are you sure you didn't imagine it?"

Levi clenched his fists, trying to keep his anger in check. "I even found documents detailing the experiments. But I had to leave them behind when I heard someone coming. I didn't have time to grab them."

Ramy shook his head, still not convinced. "Levi, it's hard to believe something like this could be happening right under our noses. How could no one else know about it?"

Kellie looked at Levi sympathetically. "Maybe you were just imagining things, Levi. It's been a tough week. Maybe the stress got to you."

Levi's face turned red with frustration. "I'm not imagining things! I know what I saw. Why won't you believe me?"

The disbelief in his friends' eyes made Levi feel isolated and alone. He had hoped they would support him, but their skepticism was a heavy blow. He stood up abruptly, his emotions boiling over.

"You know what? Forget it. I'll figure this out on my own," Levi snapped, walking away from the oak tree, leaving Kellie and Ramy behind, feeling hurt and confused.

Kellie and Ramy watched Levi Walk away, their hearts heavy with guilt and confusion. "Maybe we were too harsh on him," Kellie whispered, her eyes welling up with tears.

Ramy sighed, running a hand through his hair. "I don't know, Kellie. It just sounds so far-fetched. But I hate seeing him like this."

Determined to make things right, Kellie stood up. "We need to talk to him. Even if it sounds crazy, he's, our friend. He needs us."

They found Levi sitting alone on a bench near the school, his head in his hands. Kellie approached him slowly. "Levi, we're sorry. We didn't mean to make you feel like we don't care."

Levi looked up; his eyes red from crying. "It's not just that you didn't believe me. It's that you didn't even try to understand."

Kellie sat down next to him, placing a comforting hand on his shoulder. "We do want to understand, Levi. It's just... hard to wrap our heads around

3
The Disappearance

The next week, Kellie and Ramy arrived at school, but something felt off. Levi's usual spot in class was empty. At first, they thought he might be late, but as the day went on, there was still no sign of him.

During lunch, Kellie frowned. "Have you seen Levi today?"

Ramy shook his head, a look of concern crossing his face. "No, and it's not like him to miss school without telling us. I'm starting to get worried."

Kellie nodded. "Me too. We need to find out what's going on."

Over the next few days, Levi's absence continued, and neither Kellie nor Ramy had heard from him. Determined to find out what was happening, they decided to visit his house after school.

Kellie and Ramy walked up to Levi's front door and knocked. After a moment, Levi's mother, Mrs. Jennfier, answered, looking tired and stressed.

"Hello, Mrs. Jennfier," Kellie began cautiously. "We're Levi's friends. We noticed he hasn't been at school and were wondering if everything is okay."

Mrs. Jennfier sighed and invited them in. "Please, come in. I'm afraid things have been difficult lately."

As they sat down in the modest living room, Mrs. Jennfier explained the situation. "I recently lost my job at the bookshop. Without that income, I can't afford to pay Levi's school fees anymore. That's why he hasn't been going."

Kellie and Ramy exchanged shocked glances. "We had no idea," Kellie said softly. "Why didn't Levi tell us?"

Mrs. Jennfier smiled sadly. "He didn't want to burden you. He's been trying to stay strong, but I know it's been hard on him."

Ramy leaned forward, determination in his eyes. "We need to help him. There has to be something we can do."

After talking with Mrs. Jennfier, Kellie and Ramy asked if they could see Levi. She nodded and led them to his room. They knocked gently on the door.

"Levi? It's Kellie and Ramy. Can we come in?"

Levi's muffled voice replied, "Yeah, come in."

They entered to find Levi sitting on his bed, looking defeated. When he saw his friends, his eyes widened in surprise. "What are you guys doing here?"

Kellie sat next to him. "We were worried about you. Your mom told us what's been going on."

Ramy nodded. "Why didn't you tell us, man? We're your friends. We could have helped."

Levi looked down, ashamed. "I didn't want to be a burden. I didn't know what to do."

Kellie put a hand on Levi's shoulder. "You're not a burden, Levi. We're a team, remember? We face everything together."

Ramy smiled. "Yeah, and we'll figure something out. Maybe we can help you with school stuff or find a way to get you back to class."

Levi felt a wave of relief wash over him. "Thanks, guys. I don't know what I'd do without you."

Kellie grinned. "You'll never have to find out. We're in this together."

Levi's expression softened, but a flicker of concern remained in his eyes. "There's something else. It's not just about the school fees. I'm still upset about what I saw under the swimming pool. I know it sounds crazy, but I saw those kids and the experiments... and the principal."

Ramy and Kellie exchanged glances. Kellie spoke first. "Levi, we believe you saw something. Maybe we just don't understand it yet. But right now, let's focus on helping you with school. We'll figure out the rest together."

Levi's eyes filled with tears. "It's just... everything feels so overwhelming. My mom losing her job, not being able to go to school, and then no one believing me about what I saw."

Ramy leaned in. "We're here for you, Levi. We'll help your mom find a new job, get you back to school, and we'll get to the bottom of what's going on at the pool. But you have to trust us and let us help."

Levi nodded slowly, wiping away a tear. "Okay. I trust you guys. Thanks for being here for me."

Kellie hugged him tightly. "Always, Levi. We'll get through this. Together."

Ramy added, "And remember, no matter what happens, we're your friends. We'll figure it all out, step by step."

Levi managed a small smile. "Thanks, Ramy. Thanks, Kellie. I really appreciate it."

As they left Levi's house, Kellie and Ramy felt a renewed sense of purpose. They knew they had a lot of work ahead, but with their friendship and determination, they believed they could help Levi

Kellie and Ramy sat under the oak tree, brainstorming ways to help Levi's mother find a new job. "We could visit all the bookshop owners in town and ask if they have any openings," Kellie suggested.

Ramy nodded. "That's a good start. We need to do something."

The next day, they visited several bookshops, explaining Mrs. Jennfier' situation and asking if they had any available positions. Unfortunately, they were met with sympathetic but firm rejections.

Feeling discouraged, Kellie and Ramy decided to ask their own parents for help. "Maybe our parents can come up with something," Ramy said hopefully.

However, both sets of parents were unable to offer any concrete solutions. They expressed their sympathy but couldn't provide the help that Mrs. Jennfier needed.

Sitting back under the oak tree, Kellie sighed. "We're running out of options, Ramy."

Ramy thought for a moment. "What about Lilly and Freddy's parents? They're rich and might be able to help."

Kellie frowned. "You really think they'd help us? Lilly and Freddy hate us."

Ramy shrugged. "It's worth a try. Desperate times, right?"

Despite their doubts, Kellie and Ramy decided to visit Lilly and Freddy's home. They rang the doorbell and were surprised when Mrs. Collins, Lilly and Freddy's mother, answered the door, looking visibly stressed.

"Hello, Mrs. Collins," Kellie began hesitantly. "We're Kellie and Ramy, Levi's friends. We were hoping to talk to you about something."

Mrs. Collins invited them in, but it was clear that something was wrong. The usually immaculate house was in disarray, and the atmosphere was tense.

As they sat down, Kellie noticed Matthew, a policeman, Freddy father in the next room, speaking urgently on the phone. The snippets of conversation they overheard were chilling.

"Yes, it's about the child trafficking ring... My own daughter... disabled... younger sister of Lilly and Freddy."

Ramy's eyes widened in shock, and he quickly nudged Kellie. They exchanged a glance, both realizing the gravity of the situation. It was clear that Matthew was talking about something deeply personal and serious.

Kellie and Ramy decided not to ask for help after seeing the distress in the Collins household. "We're really sorry to bother you, Mrs. Collins. We just wanted to check if you might know of any job openings for Levi's mom. But we can see now isn't a good time," Kellie said gently.

Mrs. Collins gave them a tired smile. "Thank you for understanding. We're dealing with some family issues right now. But I appreciate your concern."

As they left the house, Ramy whispered, "Did you hear what I heard? About child trafficking and Lilly and Freddy's sister?"

Kellie nodded, her face pale. "It all fits. Levi was right. We need to do something, but we can't tell anyone yet. No one will believe us without proof."

4
Friends Found in the Face of Hardship

Kellie and Ramy knew they had to approach Lilly and Freddy delicately. Despite their rocky history, it was clear that both families were going through difficult times, and empathy was needed more than ever. They decided to start with small, casual conversations at school, gradually building a bridge of understanding.

One afternoon, during recess, they found Lilly and Freddy sitting by themselves on a bench, looking lost in thought. Ramy nudged Kellie and nodded towards them. "Now's our chance," he whispered.

Kellie took a deep breath and walked over, Ramy following close behind. "Hey, Lilly, Freddy," she began softly. "Mind if we join you?"

Lilly looked up, surprised but too tired to argue. "Sure, whatever," she muttered.

Ramy sat down next to Freddy, who was staring at the ground. "We just wanted to check in," he said. "You guys seemed... different lately."

Freddy glanced at Ramy, then away. "Yeah, well, things have been tough," he admitted reluctantly.

Kellie nodded, her voice gentle. "We heard a bit from your mom. We just wanted to let you know we're here if you need to talk."

Lilly hesitated, then sighed. "It's about our sister, Emily. She's disabled and... she's missing."

Kellie's heart ached. "I'm so sorry, Lilly. That's terrible."

Freddy finally looked up; his eyes filled with pain. "It happened a few weeks ago. We were at the park, and one moment she was there, the next she was gone. It's been a nightmare ever since."

Ramy nodded, his tone sincere. "That sounds really hard. I can't imagine what you're going through."

Lilly's eyes welled up with tears. "Emily means everything to us. She's the sweetest, most loving person. Our parents have been falling apart without her. They're doing everything they can to find her, but it's like she vanished into thin air."

Freddy's voice broke. "We used to tease you guys because... well, I don't even know why anymore. It seems so stupid now. All we want is for Emily to come home."

Kellie reached out, placing a comforting hand on Lilly's shoulder. "We're really sorry you're going through this. If there's anything we can do to help, just let us know."

Ramy added, "We may not have always gotten along, but we're all in this together now. Let's be friends and support each other through this."

Lilly wiped her tears and managed a small smile. "Thanks, Kellie. Thanks, Ramy. We could really use some friends right now."

Freddy nodded, his expression softening. "Yeah, thanks. It means a lot."

Kellie and Ramy exchanged a glance, feeling a new sense of camaraderie. They knew that by standing together, they could face the challenges ahead with a stronger, united front.

Over the next few days, the new friendship between Kellie, Ramy, Lilly, and Freddy began to grow. They spent more time together, talking about their lives and supporting each other through their struggles.

At lunch, they sat together under the oak tree, sharing stories and laughter. Ramy, ever the joker, managed to lighten the mood with his humor, while Kellie offered a steady source of compassion and understanding.

One afternoon, as they walked home from school, Freddy opened up about his feelings. "I never thought I'd say this, but it feels good to have friends like you guys. We've been so focused on finding Emily that we forgot what it's like to just... be kids."

Lilly nodded. "Yeah, it's been hard. But knowing we have you guys to lean on makes it a bit easier."

Kellie smiled warmly. "That's what friends are for. We're here for you, no matter what."

Ramy grinned. "And don't worry, we'll find a way to bring Emily back. Together."

As they parted ways, Kellie and Ramy felt a renewed sense of hope. Despite the difficulties they faced, their growing friendship with Lilly and Freddy made them stronger. They knew that by supporting each other, they could overcome any obstacle.

The new friendship between Kellie, Ramy, Lilly, and Freddy was growing stronger every day. As they spent more time together, Freddy and Lilly began to reflect on their past behavior towards Levi. Guilt gnawed at them, especially now that they understood what it meant to suffer.

One afternoon, during recess, they all sat under the oak tree, enjoying the shade and each other's company. Freddy, who had been unusually quiet, finally spoke up.

"I've been thinking a lot lately," he began, looking down at his hands. "About how I used to treat Levi."

Lilly nodded; her expression somber. "Me too. We were awful to him. I feel so guilty now."

Kellie and Ramy exchanged a glance, sensing a significant moment was about to unfold.

Freddy took a deep breath and continued. "When we teased Levi, it was like we didn't see him as a person with feelings. We just saw someone different and picked on him because of it. But now, with everything happening to us... I get it. I know how it feels to be scared and hurt."

Lilly's eyes welled up with tears. "I remember how we laughed at him because of his limp. I thought it was funny at the time, but it was cruel. And now, thinking about Emily and how vulnerable she is... I feel so ashamed."

Ramy placed a hand on Freddy's shoulder. "It takes a lot of courage to admit that, Freddy. The important thing is that you've realized it and want to make things right."

Kellie nodded. "Levi will appreciate hearing this from you. It means a lot to him that you've changed."

The next day after school, Kellie, Ramy, Lilly, and Freddy decided to visit Levi at his home. They walked to his house, feeling nervous but determined to make amends. When they arrived, Kellie knocked on the door.

Mrs. Jennfier answered, looking surprised to see them. "Hello, kids. What brings you here?"

"Hi, Mrs. Jennfier," Kellie said politely. "We were wondering if we could talk to Levi. It's important."

Mrs. Jennfier smiled warmly. "Of course, come in. He's in his room."

They followed her inside and made their way to Levi's room. Kellie knocked gently. "Levi? It's us. Can we come in?"

Levi's muffled voice replied, "Yeah, come in."

They entered to find Levi sitting on his bed, looking surprised to see Lilly and Freddy with Kellie and Ramy. "What are you guys doing here?"

Freddy stepped forward; his voice shaky. "We need to talk to you, Levi. We've been thinking a lot about how we treated you, and we want to apologize."

Levi looked at them curiously but nodded. "Okay, what's up?"

Lilly took a deep breath, her eyes full of emotion. "Levi, we're really sorry for how we treated you. We were wrong to tease you and make you feel bad. We were going through our own stuff, but that's no excuse. We were just being mean."

Freddy continued, "We didn't understand what it felt like to be on the receiving end of that kind of treatment. But now, with everything happening in our lives, we get it. And we're really sorry. We want to make it right if you'll let us."

Levi was taken aback by their sincerity. He looked at Kellie and Ramy, who both nodded encouragingly. He then turned back to Lilly and Freddy.

"I appreciate you guys saying this," Levi said slowly. "It really hurt when you teased me, and I felt so alone. But seeing you both now, I can tell you really mean it. And that means a lot to me."

Lilly wiped away a tear. "We really do, Levi. We want to be better friends to you."

Freddy added, "We know it might take time, but we hope we can earn your trust."

Levi smiled, a weight lifting off his shoulders. "I'd like that. It's not going to be easy, but I'm willing to give it a try."

Kellie and Ramy beamed with pride. "This is what friends do," Kellie said. "We support each other and help each other grow."

Ramy grinned. "Yeah, and now we're all in this together. Stronger than ever."

After their heartfelt conversation and newfound friendship, Kellie felt it was time to share the painful truth about Freddy's sister, Emily, with Levi. They all sat in Levi's room, the atmosphere growing somber.

Kellie took a deep breath and looked at Levi. "Levi, there's something else you need to know. It's about Freddy and Lilly's sister, Emily."

Levi's curiosity piqued. "What about her?"

Freddy glanced at Kellie, giving her a nod to continue. "Emily is missing. She disappeared a few weeks ago while they were at the park. Their family has been devastated ever since."

Levi's eyes widened with shock and sympathy. "I'm so sorry, Freddy. That must be incredibly hard."

Freddy nodded, his voice cracking. "It's been a nightmare. We've been doing everything we can to find her, but it's like she vanished without a trace."

The room fell silent, the weight of the situation sinking in. Levi's mind raced as he connected the dots. Suddenly, he stood up, his expression one of determination and realization.

"Kellie, Ramy, Freddy, Lilly... I think I know who might be behind Emily's disappearance," Levi said, his voice steady despite the whirlwind of emotions.

Everyone looked at Levi, puzzled. "What do you mean?" Kellie asked.

Levi took a deep breath. "Remember the underground facility I told you about? The one beneath the swimming pool? I saw kids there—lots of them. They were being held against their will. And now, with what you've told me about Emily, I think she might be one of them."

Freddy's face turned pale. "You think my sister is down there? In that place?"

Levi nodded. "It's possible. I saw things that were hard to believe, but it's starting to make sense now. The people running that facility might be behind her disappearance and possibly other missing children."

Lilly, who had been quiet, finally spoke. "But why would they take Emily? What are they doing with these kids?"

Levi looked at her, his expression grave. "From what I saw, it looks like they're using them for experiments. It's horrifying, but it fits with everything we've been hearing."

Freddy's hands clenched into fists. "We have to find her. We have to get her out of there."

Ramy placed a calming hand on Freddy's shoulder. "We will, Freddy. But we need to be smart about it. We can't just rush in without a plan."

Levi nodded. "Exactly. We need to gather more information and figure out how to expose this place without putting ourselves or the kids in more danger."

After everyone left, Levi couldn't shake off the sense of urgency and fear for Emily and the other children. Determined to find more information, he sat down at his desk and opened his laptop. He started searching for news articles about missing children in their area.

Hours passed as Levi read through countless articles, each one adding to the growing list of names and faces. He discovered that out of the 100 children who had gone missing recently, 5 to 10 of them were from his own school. The realization made his stomach churn.

The investigations into these disappearances had all reached dead ends. No leads, no suspects, no answers. It was as if the children had simply vanished into thin air. Levi's frustration grew, but so did his determination.

He knew that the authorities might not believe a group of kids, especially with such an outlandish story. But he also knew that they couldn't give up. Emily's life, and the lives of many others, depended on it.

Levi closed his laptop and leaned back in his chair, deep in thought. They needed a concrete plan, and they needed to act fast. As he stared at the ceiling, his mind began to formulate a strategy. The first step was to get everyone on board and gather as much evidence as possible.

5
Missing of Kellie

The next day at school, Ellie, Ramy, Lilly, and Freddy gathered under the old oak tree at the edge of the playground. The tree's wide branches provided a canopy of shade, creating a secluded spot where they could talk freely.

The four friends sat on the roots; their faces serious as they discussed the mysterious events surrounding the school swimming pool.

"Why would there be something so strange under the pool?" Ramy asked, scratching his head. "It doesn't make any sense."

Freddy, usually the jokester of the group, was uncharacteristically quiet. He glanced at Lilly, who gave him an encouraging nod before he began to speak.

"Well, maybe there is something down there," Freddy said, his voice trembling slightly. "My parents always said there are things we don't understand. Hidden things."

Lilly took a deep breath, her eyes welling up with tears. "My parents...they were so happy when Emily was born," she said softly. "Even though she was disabled, they loved her so much. They always tried to hide their sorrow and show only happiness to her."

Freddy put an arm around Lilly's shoulders. "Emily was so special to them. They used to tell us stories about how she could see things we couldn't, like she had a special connection to another world."

Ramy and Ellie listened intently, their own eyes beginning to water. The emotion in Lilly's voice brought tears to their eyes. Ramy wiped his face with his sleeve, trying to stay strong.

"That's so sad," Ellie whispered. "I wish there was something we could do to help."

Ellie nodded, her determination growing stronger. "We'll figure it out, somehow. There has to be a way."

But even as she said it, Ellie couldn't help but feel a pang of hopelessness. How were they supposed to uncover the secrets of the swimming pool when they didn't even know where to start?

The school bell rang, signaling the end of another long day. Freddy, Lilly, Ramy, and Kellie gathered under their usual spot, the big oak tree in the schoolyard. The tension was palpable; Levi's absence weighed heavily on their minds.

"We have to find out if Levi's telling the truth about that hidden door," Kellie said, her voice resolute. "We owe it to him, especially after everything he's been through."

Freddy nodded; his expression serious. "Yeah, we need to see it for ourselves. If there's really a hidden facility down there, we need to find it and figure out what to do next."

Ramy added, "But we need to be careful. We don't know what we're dealing with."

The friends agreed to meet at the swimming pool later in the evening, as it was open for extra hours for students interested in extra swimming practice.

Later that evening, the group sneaked into the school swimming pool. The water shimmered under the dim lights, casting eerie reflections on the walls. The pool area was quiet, with only a few other students practicing their laps.

Kellie took a deep breath. "Alright, let's spread out and search the entire pool. Remember, we need to go as deep as possible."

They nodded and jumped into the water, their movements creating ripples that disturbed the calm surface. Ramy, Freddy, and Lilly swam around the shallow and medium depths, feeling along the walls and floor for any hidden mechanisms or unusual features.

Kellie, determined to leave the surface and go deeper, ventured deeper than the others. The water grew colder and the pressure increased as she descended. She squinted through her goggles, searching the murky depths for any sign of the hidden door Levi had mentioned.

Minutes turned into what felt like hours. The group reconvened at the edge of the pool, their expressions a mix of disappointment and worry.

"I didn't find anything," Ramy said, shaking his head.

"Me neither," Freddy added.

Lilly sighed. "Nothing here either."

Just as they were about to give up, they realized Kellie was still underwater. Concern etched on their faces, they peered into the pool, hoping to catch a glimpse of their friend.

Kellie swam deeper, her determination unwavering. She felt along the cold tiles at the bottom of the pool, her fingers searching for any irregularities. Just when she thought she might have to resurface, her hand brushed against something metallic and cold. She pressed harder, and the floor beneath her shifted slightly, revealing a hidden door.

Her heart raced as she pulled the lever, and the door slowly opened. A current of water pulled her inside, and before she knew it, she was tumbling through a dark tunnel. She landed in a dimly lit room, gasping for breath.

Suddenly, she heard footsteps and hushed voices. She tried to hide, but it was too late. Strong hands grabbed her from behind, and she was dragged deeper into the underground facility.

Back at the pool, Freddy, Lilly, and Ramy were growing increasingly worried. "Where is she?" Freddy asked, panic creeping into his voice.

"We need to find her," Lilly said, her eyes wide with fear.

They dove back into the water, frantically searching for any sign of Kellie. After what felt like an eternity, they resurfaced, their faces etched with despair.

"She's not here," Ramy said, his voice breaking. "What are we going to do?"

Freddy clenched his fists, tears welling up in his eyes. "We have to tell someone. We need help."

They quickly climbed out of the pool and ran to find Coach Harper. Bursting into his office, they breathlessly explained what had happened.

"Coach, we can't find Kellie!" Freddy exclaimed. "She was underwater, and now she's gone!"

Coach Harper's face paled. "Stay here. I'll get help." He ran towards the pool, gathering other staff members to assist in the search.

The minutes dragged on as the group of friends huddled together, their minds racing with fear and worry. The staff combed every inch of the pool, but there was no sign of Kellie.

After what felt like an eternity, Coach Harper returned, his expression grim. "We've searched everywhere. There's no sign of her."

Lilly broke down in tears, and Freddy hugged her tightly, his own tears flowing freely. Ramy stared at the pool, feeling a deep sense of hopelessness.

"We'll keep looking," Coach Harper said, trying to reassure them. "We'll find her."

But as the night wore on and the search continued, the friends couldn't shake the feeling that something terrible had happened to Kellie. And they were right. Somewhere beneath the pool, in a dark, hidden facility, Kellie was trapped, waiting for a chance to escape.

Kellie struggled against the grip of the guards, her heart pounding with fear and adrenaline. The dimly lit corridors of the underground facility were lined with cold, metallic walls, casting eerie shadows as they moved. She was dragged through a labyrinth of hallways, each turn taking her deeper into the heart of the facility.

Finally, they reached a large, imposing door. The guards pushed it open, revealing a spacious room filled with high-tech equipment and monitors displaying various parts of the facility.

In the center of the room stood a tall figure, the leader of the facility, with an aura of authority and menace.

The leader turned to face Kellie, a sinister smile spreading across their face. "Ah, Kellie. We missed you during your first visit. It seems we overlooked you somehow."

Kellie's eyes widened in shock. She opened her mouth to correct the leader, but then thought better of it. If they knew it was Levi who had been here before, it might put him in danger. "Y-yes, it seems so," she stammered.

The leader chuckled, the sound cold and chilling. "Of course. We know everything that happens in our facility. But let's not dwell on that. Tell me, Kellie, have you mentioned our little secret to anyone?"

Kellie swallowed hard, her voice trembling. "Yes, I did. But no one believed me."

The leader laughed, a cruel, mocking sound. "How fortunate for us. It seems your warnings fell on deaf ears. No one will come looking for you."

Kellie felt a surge of anger and fear. "What do you want with me?"

The leader's smile faded, replaced by a look of cold calculation. "You will join the other children we have here. Guards, take her away and lock her up. We have plans for her."

The guards tightened their grip on Kellie and began dragging her away. She struggled, her mind racing with thoughts of escape and fear for her friends. As they led her through more dimly lit corridors, the reality of her situation set in. She was trapped in a nightmarish facility, with no idea how to get out or how to warn the others.

Finally, they reached a room filled with other children, their faces pale and scared. The guards shoved her inside and locked the door behind her. Kellie looked around, her heart sinking as she realized the enormity of what she and her friends had uncovered.

She was determined to find a way out and save the others, but for now, she was just another prisoner in the underground facility.

...

Back at the pool, As the night wore on and the search continued, word of Kellie's disappearance spread through the school. The principal, Mr. Nicholas, gathered the entire school management team and informed Mr. Daniel, Kellie's father, about the situation. His face turned ashen as he listened to the news, his hands trembling.

Mr. Daniel rushed to the school, his heart pounding with fear. "Where is my daughter?" he demanded, his voice shaking.

"We're doing everything we can to find her, Mr. Daniel," Mr. Nicholas said, trying to calm him. "We've called the police, and they'll be here soon."

Within minutes, the police arrived at the school, led by Matthew, Freddy's father. His stern face softened when he saw the distressed students and staff.

"Alright, everyone," Matthew said, taking charge. "We need to gather all the information we can. Mr. Daniel, can you tell us what happened?"

Mr. Daniel, his voice thick with emotion, recounted the events as best as he could. "She was last seen swimming with her friends. They said she went underwater and never came back up."

Matthew nodded, turning to his team. "Spread out and search the entire area. Look for any clues that might tell us where she went."

The police officers began a thorough investigation of the pool and surrounding areas. They questioned students, staff, and anyone who might have seen something unusual. Freddy, Lilly, and Ramy were asked to describe exactly what had happened.

"We were swimming," Ramy said, his voice trembling. "Kellie went deeper than the rest of us. We saw her go down, but she didn't come back up. We searched everywhere, but there was no sign of her."

Lilly added, her voice barely above a whisper, "We tried to find her. We really did. But she just... disappeared."

Matthew listened carefully; his brow furrowed with concern. "Thank you, kids. You've been very brave. We'll do everything we can to find her."

Hours passed, and the investigation continued. The police scoured the pool area, manually checking for any hidden compartments or unusual features. They interviewed more witnesses, and searched every corner of the school grounds.

Despite their efforts, no clues emerged. It was as if Kellie had vanished into thin air.

Matthew gathered the school management, Mr. Daniel, and the friends once more. "I'm sorry to say that we haven't found anything yet. We'll keep investigating, but it might take time."

Mr. Daniel's face crumpled with despair. "Please, find my daughter. She's all I have."

Matthew placed a reassuring hand on his shoulder. "Mr. Daniel, I understand how you feel. My own daughter is also missing, and I know the pain you're going through. I promise you; we will do everything in our power to find Kellie. We'll keep looking until we find her."

As the night turned into early morning, the police continued their search, but the sense of dread grew heavier.

Freddy, Lilly, and Ramy stayed close together, their hearts aching with worry for their friend. The uncertainty of Kellie's fate hung over them like a dark cloud, but they vowed to keep hope alive and support each other through the ordeal.

The Investigation Takes a Different Turn

The next morning, Detective Matthew Collins gathered his team for a briefing. The lack of evidence from the pool area was frustrating, and he needed to consider other possibilities. "Alright, everyone, let's re-evaluate our approach. We might be missing something. Maybe Kellie isn't in the pool area. She could be somewhere else in the school."

His team nodded, understanding the need to explore all avenues. Matthew turned to the kids. "Freddy, Lilly, Ramy, I need to ask you some more questions. Could you please come with me?"

The three friends followed Matthew to a quiet room. "I know you've been through a lot, but I need you to think hard. Did you notice anything unusual in the school, any place Kellie might have gone?"

Ramy shook his head. "No, we were all focused on the pool. We didn't see anything strange."

Freddy, his voice wavering, added, "She was determined to find something underwater. She wouldn't just leave."

Lilly nodded in agreement. "Kellie wouldn't give up like that. She must be in the pool area."

Matthew sighed, sensing their disappointment. "I understand, but we have to consider every possibility. If there's a chance, she's somewhere else, we need to look there too."

He stood up, addressing his team. "Let's expand the search to other parts of the school. Check every room, every closet, and any place someone could hide."

As the police began searching other areas of the school, Freddy, Lilly, and Ramy watched with growing frustration. "They're wasting time," Ramy muttered. "Kellie is in the pool area. We know it."

Freddy clenched his fists, feeling helpless. "We need to keep looking at ourselves. We can't just sit here."

Lilly, her eyes filled with determination, said, "We will. We'll find her."

Despite their determination, the friends couldn't shake the feeling of disappointment as the investigation seemed to be moving in a different direction.

They knew Kellie was in danger, and every moment counted. But for now, all they could do was wait and hope the police would find some clue to lead them to their friend.

The next day, the news of Kellie's disappearance had spread throughout the school, casting a shadow over the students. Andrew and Brittany, who had been on a week-long school leave, returned to find the atmosphere somber and filled with whispers of concern.

As they walked through the halls, they noticed the worried faces of younger friends. Brittany's heart sank, and Andrew's usually confident stride slowed as they approached their friends.

"What's going on?" Andrew asked, his voice laced with worry.

Freddy looked up; his eyes red-rimmed from lack of sleep. "It's Kellie. She's missing."

Brittany's face went pale, and tears welled up in her eyes. "Missing? How? When?"

Lilly, her own voice shaky, explained, "It happened while we were at the swimming pool. She went underwater and never came back up. We've searched everywhere, but there's no sign of her."

Brittany's tears spilled over, and she sobbed uncontrollably. Andrew put a comforting arm around her, his own expression grim. "How could this happen?" he muttered, his mind racing.

Andrew and Brittany Learn the Mystery of the Underwater Swimming Pool

Later that day, Andrew and Brittany sat with Freddy, Ramy, and Lilly under the old oak tree. Brittany had calmed down somewhat, but the worry and fear still lingered in her eyes.

"Tell us everything," Andrew said, his voice steady but urgent. "We need to know what happened."

Ramy nodded, taking a deep breath. "It started with Levi. He told us about something he saw under the swimming pool. He said there was a hidden door, and he saw children being held there."

Andrew's eyes widened in shock. "What? Why didn't he tell us sooner?"

Lilly interjected, "He did tell us, but we didn't believe him at first. We thought it was just his imagination. But then we started to notice strange things happening around the pool."

Freddy continued, "Kellie wanted to investigate. She thought Levi might be onto something, so we decided to check it out. That's when she disappeared."

Brittany, her voice trembling, asked, "What exactly did Levi see?"

Ramy explained, "He said he saw an underground facility with children being held there for some kind of experiments. It sounded crazy, but Kellie believed him and wanted to find out the truth."

Andrew shook his head in disbelief. "This is unbelievable. How could something like that be happening right under our noses?"

Freddy, his expression serious, added, "We didn't believe him at first either, but now... now we don't know what to think. Kellie wouldn't just vanish. Something's going on, and we need to figure out what."

Brittany wiped her tears, her resolve hardening. "We have to find her. We can't just sit here and do nothing."

Andrew nodded; his jaw set with determination. "You're right. We need to dig deeper and find out what happened to Kellie. If there's any chance Levi was right, we have to investigate."

Ramy, Freddy, and Lilly nodded in agreement, their spirits bolstered by the support of their older friends. Together, they vowed to uncover the truth and bring Kellie back.

After school, Andrew, Brittany, Freddy, Lilly, and Ramy made their way to Levi's house. Their hearts were heavy with the news they had to share. As they approached the door, Andrew knocked gently.

Levi's mother opened the door, her face etched with worry. "Hello, kids. Levi's in his room. He's been really down lately."

They nodded, thanking her, and made their way to Levi's room. Inside, they found him sitting on his bed, staring blankly at the floor. When he saw his friends, his eyes brightened momentarily but quickly dimmed as he sensed their serious expressions.

"Levi, we need to talk," Ramy said softly.

Levi looked up; concern etched on his face. "What's going on?"

Brittany took a deep breath. "It's Kellie. She's... she's missing."

Levi's eyes widened in shock. "What? How? When?"

Freddy explained, "It happened at the swimming pool. She went underwater and never came back up. We've searched everywhere, but there's no sign of her."

Levi's face contorted with sorrow and anger. "No... this can't be happening. Kellie... she always looked out for me. She believed me when no one else did."

Lilly placed a comforting hand on Levi's shoulder. "We know, Levi. And we're going to find her. We just need to figure out how."

Levi's mind raced, memories of Kellie flooding back. "She was like an elder sister to me. I remember when we first met. I was new and scared, and she stood up for me when some kids were picking on me because of my leg. She said I was stronger than I knew and made me feel like I belonged."

Brittany's eyes filled with tears as Levi continued, "And when I struggled with my schoolwork, she would stay late to help me. She never let anyone make me feel less because of my disability. She always told me I was special and that I could do anything I set my mind to."

Levi clenched his fists, his voice shaking with emotion. "We have to find her. She would do the same for any of us."

Andrew, his voice firm but gentle, said, "We will, Levi. But we need to be smart about this. We need to get help."

Freddy nodded. "We think we should tell my dad, Matthew. He's a police officer. If anyone can help us, it's him."

Levi took a deep breath, trying to steady himself. "Okay. Let's go. We need to do this for Kellie."

As they prepared to leave, Levi's mother appeared in the doorway. "Levi, are you okay?"

Levi nodded; his expression determined. "Mom, we need to talk to Freddy's dad. He might be able to help us find Kellie."

She nodded, understanding the urgency in his voice. "Be careful, Levi. And come back home if you need anything."

Levi gathered all the proof he had meticulously collected over the past months, including newspaper clippings and printouts of missing children's reports from across the country.

He also included detailed notes about the children who had gone missing from their school in earlier days. Determined and hopeful, he clutched the evidence tightly, ready to present it to Freddy's father, Matthew.

The group left Levi's house; their hearts heavy but united in their mission. They walked in silence, each lost in their thoughts and memories of Kellie. The bond they shared grew stronger as they faced this new challenge together, determined to uncover the truth and bring Kellie back safely.

6
Revealing the Depths

Levi, Ramy, and their elder friends Andrew and Brittany, met with Lilly and Freddy at Freddy's house. They gathered around the kitchen table, waiting anxiously for Freddy's father, Matthew, to join them. When Matthew entered the room, the kids looked at each other, their faces serious.

"Mr. Matthew, we need to talk to you about something very important," Levi began, his voice steady but urgent.

Matthew, a logical and reasoning man who had seen many things in his years as a police officer, nodded. "Alright, Levi. What's going on?"

Levi took a deep breath and started explaining. "It all started when I found something strange under the swimming pool. I saw a hidden door and children being held there."

Matthew raised an eyebrow, clearly skeptical. "Levi, that sounds far-fetched. Are you sure you weren't imagining things?"

Andrew interjected, "Mr. Matthew, we didn't believe it at first either. But then Kellie went missing, and we have reason to believe it's connected."

Brittany added, "Please, just hear us out. Levi has gathered a lot of information about missing children, not just from our school but from all over the country."

Matthew sighed, not wanting to disappoint the kids but clearly struggling to believe their story. "Alright, show me what you have."

Levi spread out the documents and newspaper clippings he had collected over the past months. "These are reports of missing children. Some of them went missing from our school, and others from different places across the country. There's a pattern."

Matthew reviewed the information, his initial skepticism giving way to shock as he began to connect the dots. "This is...

troubling," he admitted. "But a hidden door under the swimming pool? That's hard to believe."

Levi, determined, continued, "I know it sounds unbelievable, but it's true. We have to investigate. Please, Mr. Matthew, you have to trust me."

Matthew, seeing the earnestness in Levi's eyes, nodded slowly. "Alright, I'll start looking into this. But understand, I need to follow procedure. This will have to be approved by my superiors."

After making a few calls and explaining the situation, Matthew managed to get the necessary approvals. Despite some of his colleagues making fun of the mysterious story, he was determined to follow through.

The next day, a team of police officers arrived at the school, much to the surprise of the staff and students. Matthew directed the operation, determined to find out if there was any truth to Levi's claims.

"We're going to drain the swimming pool," Matthew announced, earning puzzled looks from his team.

One of the officers chuckled, "You really think there's a hidden door down there, Matt?"

Matthew, ignoring the comment, replied, "We're following a lead. Let's get to work."

The team set up the equipment to drain the pool. The students watched from a distance, whispering among themselves, unsure of what to make of the situation.

Freddy, Lilly, Ramy, Andrew, Brittany, and Levi stood together, hope and anxiety mingling in their hearts. As the water level lowered, they held their breath, waiting to see if Levi's story would be validated.

The water continued to drain, inch by inch, revealing the tiles at the bottom of the pool. Everyone watched intently, the air thick with tension and anticipation.

As the police began the process of draining the swimming pool, the students and staff gathered around, curious and anxious. Principal Mr. Nicholas stood with Coach Harper and several teachers, watching the proceedings with a mix of disbelief and concern.

Coach Harper leaned over to Mr. Nicholas. "Do you really think there's something down there, Nicholas? It sounds like a wild story."

Mr. Nicholas sighed; his gaze fixed on the slowly lowering water level. "I don't know, Harper. But if there's even a chance that this could help us find Kellie, we have to take it seriously."

Nearby, a group of students whispered among themselves. "Do you think they'll find anything?" one asked.

"I don't know," another replied. "But it's kind of exciting, isn't it?"

As the water continued to drain, Levi, Ramy, Andrew, Brittany, Freddy, and Lilly stood together, their eyes wide with anticipation. Levi's heart pounded in his chest, his mind racing with memories of what he had seen.

Freddy noticed his father's intense focus and approached him cautiously. "Dad, do you really think Levi could be right?"

Matthew glanced at his son, his expression softening. "I don't know, Freddy. But Levi's evidence was compelling. We have to follow every lead."

One of the teachers, Ms. Jenkins, approached the group of kids. "What's going on here? Why is the pool being drained?"

Lilly, her voice trembling slightly, explained, "We think there might be something hidden under the pool. Something related to Kellie's disappearance."

Ms. Jenkins raised an eyebrow, clearly skeptical. "That sounds like quite a story."

Andrew stepped forward, his voice steady. "It is. But Levi saw something. We have to believe him and see this through."

Coach Harper joined the conversation, his arms crossed. "I've been coaching here for years. If there's something under that pool, I want to know about it."

Mr. Nicholas, overhearing the exchange, added, "We all do, Harper. Let's just hope this leads us to some answers."

As the water level dropped further, a hush fell over the crowd. The bottom of the pool began to emerge, revealing the intricate tile patterns. The anticipation grew thicker, and the students and staff leaned forward, eager to catch a glimpse of anything unusual.

One of the officers called out, "We're getting close! Keep your eyes peeled!"

Levi's heart raced as he scanned the emerging tiles, looking for the hidden door he had seen. Ramy, standing beside him, whispered, "Do you see it, Levi?"

"Not yet," Levi replied, his voice barely above a whisper. "But it's there. I know it is."

The tension in the air was palpable as the last few inches of water drained away. The bottom of the pool was now fully visible, but there was no immediate sign of a door or any other hidden feature.

Matthew, feeling the weight of the moment, turned to Levi. "Where exactly did you see the door, Levi?"

As the water drained completely, a sense of dread began to creep into Levi's heart. He had been so sure of what he had seen, but now, as the last few inches of water revealed the perfectly ordinary tiles of the pool bottom, doubt began to gnaw at him.

Matthew, feeling the weight of the moment, turned to Levi. "Where exactly did you see the door, Levi?"

Levi pointed to a specific section of the pool. "Over there, near the center. There's a tile that should be different from the rest."

The officers moved to the spot Levi indicated and began examining the tiles closely. The crowd held their breath, watching as the officers carefully inspected each tile.

But as they searched, no hidden door or lever was found. The tiles were just as they appeared: ordinary and unremarkable. Murmurs began to ripple through the crowd, a mixture of disappointment and skepticism.

One of the officers stood up, shaking his head. "There's nothing here, Matthew."

Matthew sighed deeply; his frustration evident. "Alright, everyone. Pack it up."

The students and staff began to disperse, their curiosity turning into whispers and side glances. Levi stood frozen, his face pale with disbelief. Ramy, Andrew, Brittany, Freddy, and Lilly gathered around him, their expressions a mix of concern and confusion.

Principal Nicholas, who had been observing quietly, finally spoke up. "Levi, maybe you were just... mistaken. Sometimes our minds play tricks on us, especially when we're under stress."

Levi's heart sank. He felt a wave of embarrassment wash over him as the reality of the situation set in. He had been so certain, but now he felt like a fool in front of everyone.

Matthew, trying to salvage some dignity, addressed the crowd. "We followed a lead, and while it didn't pan out, it was a necessary step. We'll continue the investigation."

But Levi could see the disappointment and annoyance on the faces of the other officers. He had caused a scene, and it had led to nothing. The kids at school would surely talk about this for weeks, if not months.

As the crowd began to dissipate, Levi felt the weight of their whispers and glances. He had become the subject of ridicule, and he could hear snippets of conversations mocking his claims.

"Did you hear what Levi said? A hidden door under the pool? What a joke."

"Yeah, and the police actually believed him. Can you imagine?"

Levi's face burned with humiliation. He wanted to disappear, to run away from the judgmental eyes and harsh words. His friends tried to console him, but it was no use.

Freddy, seeing his father's expression, felt a pang of guilt. "Dad, Levi was just trying to help. He didn't mean for this to happen."

Matthew placed a hand on Freddy's shoulder. "I know, son. But we have to be careful with our claims. This has put us all in a difficult position."

Levi, feeling utterly defeated, started to walk away, but Principal Nicholas called after him. "Levi, wait."

Levi turned, tears stinging his eyes. Principal Nicholas approached him, his expression softening. "Levi, I know this is hard for you. You believed in what you saw, and you were brave enough to speak up. That takes a lot of courage."

Levi shook his head, the tears now spilling over. "But I was wrong. Now everyone thinks I'm a fool."

Principal Nicholas sighed, placing a comforting hand on Levi's shoulder. "Being wrong doesn't make you a fool, Levi. It makes you human. What matters is that you tried to help. And I believe that if you keep searching for the truth, you'll find it. Don't lose hope."

Levi nodded, trying to take comfort in the principal's words. But the sting of embarrassment was still fresh, and he knew it would take time to heal.

As Levi walked away with his friends, he couldn't help but replay the events in his mind. He had been so sure, so certain. And now, he felt like everything had crumbled beneath him. But deep down, he resolved to keep searching for answers, no matter how difficult the journey might be.

7
The Shadows of Suspicion

The investigation into the mysterious swimming pool and the search for Kellie had quickly become the talk of the town. The local newspapers were filled with headlines about the school's strange events, and the story had spread like wildfire.

"School Swimming Pool Mystery: Missing Student Sparks Investigation" read one headline.

"Police Baffled by Alleged Hidden Facility Under Pool" read another.

As the town buzzed with rumors and speculation, the school administration decided to close the school for three weeks to facilitate the investigation. The usually bustling halls and playgrounds now stood silent, giving the school an eerie, deserted feel. The closure added pressure to the investigation, and Matthew found himself in a tense, almost frantic mood as he tried to make sense of the confusing and frustrating lack of progress.

Levi's Team Decides to Get Involved Directly

Levi's living room was filled with a heavy silence. Levi, Ramy, Lilly, Freddy, Andrew, and Brittany sat around the coffee table, the atmosphere thick with tension.

Levi broke the silence. "We can't just sit around and wait anymore. We need to do something to find Kellie and the other kids."

Andrew nodded. "If no one else will help, we have to take matters into our own hands."

Brittany looked hesitant, her voice trembling. "But what if something goes wrong? What if we get caught or... or worse?"

Andrew reached over and squeezed her hand reassuringly. "I know it's scary, Brittany. But we can't let fear stop us. Kellie is out there somewhere, and she's counting on us."

Brittany took a deep breath, Andrew's words giving her strength. "You're right. We can't just leave her. We have to do this."

Lilly added, "We'll be careful. We'll stick together and make sure everyone stays safe."

Freddy, trying to lighten the mood, grinned. "And besides, we're a pretty smart group. If anyone can figure this out, it's us."

The group exchanged determined looks and agreed to take action. They knew the risks, but their resolve was unwavering.

The Haunted School

The school, now closed for two weeks, stood like a ghost house and the school looked spooky. The playground, once filled with children laughing and playing, was now empty and still.

The swings moved slightly in the wind, but no one was there to use them. The classrooms were dark, with desks and chairs sitting quietly, waiting for students who wouldn't come.

The hallways were empty and quiet. Every step echoed loudly, making the silence even more noticeable. The gym, where students used to play basketball and other games, was now completely silent and dark. The whole school felt like a place from a scary story.

Windows were covered with boards, and yellow caution tape blocked off certain areas. The tape fluttered in the wind, making soft, rustling noises that added to the spooky feeling. The doors creaked loudly when opened, echoing through the empty building.

The sight of the empty school sent shivers down anyone's spine. It was hard to believe that this quiet, creepy place was once full of life and excitement. The silence and emptiness made it feel like something mysterious and scary was hiding just around the corner.

That evening, each member of Levi's team approached their parents with a carefully crafted story.

At Ramy's house, he pleaded with his parents. "Can I stay at Levi's for a few days? We're just feeling bored and lonely at home."

His parents exchanged a glance and nodded. "Alright, Ramy. Just be safe."

Lilly's parents were initially hesitant. "Are you sure you'll be, okay?"

Lilly smiled reassuringly. "Yes, I'll be with my friends."

Freddy's father, Matthew, gave him a stern lecture. "I'm trusting you to be safe, Freddy. Don't do anything reckless."

Freddy nodded. "I promise, Dad."

Andrew and Brittany received similar permissions from their parents, who thought it was a good idea for them to spend time with friends.

Planning and Plotting Different Strategies

Later that night, Levi's living room buzzed with activity. Snacks were spread out on the coffee table, creating a makeshift command center. The room was filled with a mix of nervous energy and determination.

Levi took a rough piece of paper and started sketching out the school's layout from memory, marking various facilities they were familiar with. "Here's what I remember. The swimming pool is here, and the gym is next to it. But we need the actual blueprints to find any hidden areas."

Ramy, leaning over the sketch, suggested, "We need a lookout. Someone to distract anyone who might see us. That way, the rest of us can move freely."

Brittany, still feeling a bit nervous, added, "And we have to make sure we don't get caught. What if the police or someone sees us? We can't afford to get into trouble."

Andrew, taking charge, replied, "We'll be smart about this. We'll plan every step carefully. We can do this."

Lilly nodded in agreement. "And we have to be careful. We can't afford to make any mistakes. One wrong move, and it's all over."

Levi continued, "We need to gather more information about the school's layout and construction. The blueprints should have details about any hidden areas or tunnels."

Freddy chimed in with an idea. "My dad has information about the police presence at the school. If I can get into his computer or notebooks early tomorrow morning, I can find out how many police officers are there, who they are, and their names. That way, we can plan how to distract some of them."

The group looked at Freddy, impressed. "That's a great idea," Andrew said. "If we know more about the police, it'll make our job easier."

Ramy suggested, "We should scout the area first. See what the situation is like. Brittany and I can handle that."

Brittany, feeling a mix of fear and determination, nodded. "Okay, but we have to be really careful. We can't let anyone see us."

Andrew agreed. "Good. While you two check out the outside, Freddy will gather information from his dad's notes. The rest of us will stay here and wait for you to come back."

Levi looked around at his friends. "Who's going to get into the principal's office for the blueprints?"

Andrew stepped forward. "I'll do it. I'm quick and quiet, and I know how to avoid getting caught."

Lilly expressed her concern. "Are you sure, Andrew? It's risky."

Andrew nodded confidently. "I can handle it. We don't have any other choice. We need those blueprints to know what we're dealing with."

The group continued to discuss the plan in detail, considering every possible scenario. They talked about the risks, the potential challenges, and the need for precision and stealth.

As they planned, the weight of the situation pressed down on them. They knew they were stepping into dangerous territory, but their bond and resolve to find Kellie kept them focused. They were determined to succeed, no matter what challenges lay ahead.

The Next Day

The next morning, as planned, the group split up to carry out their tasks.

Ramy and Brittany headed to the school to scout the area. They kept a low profile, observing the police presence and noting any potential entry points.

Meanwhile, Freddy went back home to gather information from his father's computer and notebooks. He knew he had to be quick and discreet, making sure his father didn't find out what he was doing.

Back at Levi's house, Andrew, Levi, and Lilly waited anxiously for their friends to return. They knew that the success of their plan depended on the information Ramy, Brittany, and Freddy could gather.

Andrew paced the room, his mind racing with possibilities. "I hope they're okay," he muttered.

Levi, trying to stay positive, replied, "They'll be fine. We just have to trust them."

Lilly nodded, though she couldn't shake the feeling of worry. "Let's just hope everything goes as planned."

As they waited, the tension in the room grew. They knew that today's efforts would be crucial in their mission to find Kellie and uncover the truth.

Ramy and Brittany Scout the School

Ramy and Brittany moved cautiously around the perimeter of the school, making sure to stay hidden from sight. They took note of everything they saw, trying to gather as much information as possible.

"Okay, there are two police officers at the main entrance," Ramy whispered, peeking around a corner.

Brittany nodded, jotting down notes in a small notebook. "I see another one patrolling near the gym. That makes three so far."

They continued their reconnaissance, moving stealthily from one hiding spot to another. They observed the movements and routines of the police officers, noting their positions and any potential blind spots.

Ramy pointed towards the back of the school. "There's a side entrance near the cafeteria. It's not guarded, but we'd have to move quickly to avoid being seen."

Brittany looked thoughtful. "If we can create a distraction at the front, it might draw the officers away from the side entrance."

Ramy nodded. "Good idea. We could use something loud, like setting off a car alarm or causing a commotion."

After making a few more observations, they decided they had enough information and headed back to Levi's house to share their findings.

Freddy Gathers Information

Meanwhile, Freddy was at home, carefully searching through his father's computer and notebooks. He found detailed notes about the police officers assigned to the school, including their names, routines, and where they were stationed.

Freddy quickly jotted down the information, making sure to note any patterns or weaknesses in their schedule. He knew this information would be crucial for their plan.

Once he had everything he needed, he carefully put his father's things back in order and headed to Levi's house to meet up with the rest of the group.

Sharing the Information

Back at Levi's house, Andrew, Levi, and Lilly waited anxiously for their friends to return. When Ramy, Brittany, and Freddy arrived, they quickly gathered around to share what they had learned.

Ramy started, "There are three police officers patrolling the school. Two at the main entrance and one near the gym. The side entrance by the cafeteria is unguarded, but we'll need a distraction to use it."

Brittany added, "If we can create a loud noise at the front, it might draw the officers away long enough for us to get inside."

Freddy handed over his notes. "I found out more about the police officers. Here are their names, schedules, and where they're stationed. We can use this to time our move perfectly."

Andrew studied the notes and the information from Ramy and Brittany. "Okay, here's what we're going to do. We'll use the side entrance near the cafeteria to get inside. Ramy and Brittany will create a distraction at the front. Freddy, you'll stay on lookout and signal us if anything changes. Levi, Lilly, and I will head to the principal's office to get the blueprints."

Levi nodded, feeling a mix of excitement and nervousness. "This is it. We're really doing this."

Lilly added, "We have to be careful and stick to the plan. One mistake and it's all over."

Andrew looked at each of them, determination in his eyes. "We can do this. Let's go over the plan again and make sure everyone knows their part."

The group huddled together, discussing the details and making sure everyone was prepared. They knew the risks, but their determination to find Kellie and uncover the truth kept them focused.

Executing the Plan

It was 5:45 PM, and the team gathered at their rendezvous point near the school. The sun was beginning to set, casting long shadows across the playground. The air was filled with nervous excitement as they prepared to execute their plan.

Ramy and Brittany made their way to a nearby telephone booth. Ramy picked up the receiver and dialed the school's main office number, putting on his best authoritative voice. "Hello, this is Officer Christopher from the police headquarters. I need to speak with the officers stationed at the school."

After a brief hold, one of the officers answered. "This is Officer Greene."

Ramy cleared his throat, trying to sound as official as possible. "Officer Greene, we have an urgent request for you and Officer Walker to report to the police headquarters immediately. There's a special recognition ceremony, and you both have been selected for a distinguished service award."

Officer Greene sounded surprised. "An award? Really?"

Ramy nodded eagerly, though the officer couldn't see him. "Yes, absolutely. It's a significant honor, and we have a beautiful gift waiting for you. Please head over as soon as possible."

Officer Greene agreed, and within minutes, both officers were seen leaving their posts and heading towards the police headquarters.

Ramy hung up the phone, turning to Brittany with a grin. "Can you believe they bought that? A beautiful gift for best works. Sounds like something from a bad TV show."

Brittany laughed. "I can't believe it either. You should be an actor."

They quickly made their way back to the rest of the team, who were hiding a safe distance from the school. "Okay, the distraction worked. Two officers are heading to the police headquarters for their 'award'," Ramy said, making air quotes.

Freddy chuckled. "I can't believe they fell for that. Nice work, Ramy."

Andrew nodded. "Alright, let's move to phase two. Freddy, you know what to do."

Freddy made his way to the side of the school and positioned himself near a window. He took out a small speaker and played a pre-recorded sound of strange, eerie noises, echoing through the hallways. The remaining officer near the gym, puzzled by the sound, moved towards the source, leaving his post.

Ramy couldn't help but laugh. "That sound is ridiculous. It's like something out of a horror movie."

The team stifled their giggles as they watched the officer slowly wander off, trying to locate the source of the noise. This was their chance.

Andrew nodded to the group. "Alright, I'm going in. Stay hidden and keep an eye out."

With the coast clear, Andrew made his way to the side entrance near the cafeteria. He moved quickly and quietly, slipping inside the school. The rest of the team, including Levi, Ramy, Lilly, and Brittany, waited anxiously a safe distance away, keeping watch for any signs of trouble.

They stayed in constant communication with quiet whispers and hand signals, the tension mounting as they waited for Andrew to return.

Andrew Searches for the Blueprints

Andrew slipped inside the school through the side entrance near the cafeteria, his heart pounding with adrenaline. The halls were eerily silent, lit only by the dim emergency lights casting long shadows. He moved quickly and quietly, making his way to the principal's office.

Once inside the office, Andrew began searching through drawers and cabinets, looking for the blueprints. He found stacks of documents, old school records, and various administrative papers. The room smelled of old paper and dust, adding to the sense of urgency.

He opened a large filing cabinet, flipping through folders labeled "School Plans" and "Construction Details." His eyes scanned each label quickly, hoping to find what he was looking for.

"Come on, come on," he muttered under his breath, feeling the pressure mounting. Time was running out, and he needed to find the blueprints before the police returned to their posts.

After several minutes of searching, he finally found a rolled-up set of blueprints labeled "School Construction Plans." He unrolled them on the principal's desk, quickly scanning the detailed drawings. There were markings and notes indicating changes made over the years.

"Yes!" Andrew whispered excitedly. He carefully rolled up the blueprints and secured them under his arm. Just as he was about to leave the office, he heard footsteps echoing down the hallway.

A Narrow Escape

Andrew's heart raced as he realized the police were returning to their positions. The eerie sound Freddy had played hadn't yielded any results, and now the officers were suspicious. He needed to find another way out without being seen.

He quickly scanned the room, his eyes landing on a small window near the ceiling. It looked just big enough for him to squeeze through. He grabbed a chair and climbed up, pushing the window open. The cold night air hit his face as he pulled himself up and through the narrow opening.

Outside, he found himself on the roof of the school. The wind whipped around him, but he knew he had to keep moving. He carefully made his way across the rooftop, looking for a safe way down.

Back on the ground, the rest of the team watched nervously as the police officers returned to their posts, looking more alert and suspicious than before.

"Where's Andrew?" Lilly whispered; her voice tinged with worry.

"He should be out by now," Levi replied, his eyes scanning the building.

Suddenly, Brittany spotted movement on the roof. "Look, there he is!"

Andrew had found a fire escape ladder at the back of the building. He climbed down quickly and quietly, clutching the blueprints tightly. As he reached the ground, he ran towards the group, trying to stay out of sight.

The Officers Return and Andrew Rejoins the Team

Just as Andrew made it back to the group, the officers who had been sent to the police headquarters returned, looking furious. They had realized they had been tricked and were not happy about it.

"Whoever made that call is in big trouble," Officer Greene muttered angrily to his partner.

The team watched from a distance, trying to stifle their laughter. "Looks like Ramy's plan worked a little too well," Freddy said, grinning.

Andrew finally reached the group, breathing heavily but smiling triumphantly. "I got it. I got the blueprints."

The team hugged him, relieved and excited. "You did it, Andrew!" Levi exclaimed.

"Let's get out of here before anyone notices us," Ramy suggested.

They quickly made their way back to Levi's house, sticking to the shadows and avoiding any potential onlookers.

8
Master Planning

Reviewing the Blueprints

Back at Levi's house, the team gathered around the living room, their excitement palpable. Andrew unrolled the blueprints on the coffee table, and they all leaned in to get a closer look.

"These show everything," Andrew explained. "This is exactly what we needed."

Levi nodded, feeling a surge of hope. "This is it. We're getting closer to finding Kellie."

Lilly pointed to a section of the blueprints. "Look, there's a tunnel entrance marked here. This might be where we need to go."

As the team began to carefully review the blueprints, excitement quickly turned to confusion. The drawings were filled with complex symbols and technical details that were hard to understand.

Ramy frowned, flipping through the pages. "I don't get it. This is so complicated."

Freddy scratched his head. "Yeah, it's like trying to read another language."

Andrew, determined, spread out several different drawings, comparing them side by side. "We're missing something. There has to be a clue here somewhere."

Brittany, who had been quietly examining an older revision of the blueprints, suddenly gasped. "Wait a minute. Look at this."

Everyone gathered around as Brittany pointed to a section of the older blueprints. "This area is different in the final drawings. They changed something major here."

Levi compared the two sets of drawings. "You're right. This whole section is missing in the newer plans."

Brittany nodded, her eyes wide with realization. "They removed something important. Look at the older version—there's a whole underground facility here."

The group stared at the detailed drawings of the underground facility, their hearts pounding with shock. It showed rooms and corridors that were clearly not part of the school's official blueprints.

Lilly's voice trembled. "This is it. This is what Levi saw. But how do we get in?"

Freddy continued to scan the blueprints, frustration mounting. "There's got to be an entrance somewhere."

Ramy flipped through another set of drawings, his eyes suddenly lighting up. "Guys, look at this!"

He pointed to a small, almost hidden marking on the blueprint. "There's an underground tunnel that starts here, inside the school grounds, and extends all the way to the supermarket on the other side of town."

Levi traced the route with his finger. "This could be our way in. If we can get to the tunnel entrance, we might be able to reach the underground facility."

Andrew nodded, feeling a surge of determination. "We need to find this tunnel entrance. It's our best shot at finding Kellie and the other kids."

Brittany, still in shock, added, "This is huge. We need to be careful and plan this out. If this facility is real, who knows what we're up against."

The team continued to pour over the blueprints, their initial confusion giving way to a renewed sense of purpose. They knew the risks were high, but their discovery had given them the breakthrough they needed.

Making Up a New Story for Parents

Back at Levi's house, the team gathered around the living room, the blueprints spread out before them. The room was filled with a sense of urgency as they prepared for their next move. Levi looked at his friends, knowing they needed a new plan to explain their extended absence from home.

Levi took a deep breath. "Guys, it's been three days since we all came to my house. Our parents are going to start asking questions. We need to come up with a new story."

Ramy nodded, understanding the seriousness of the situation. "Yeah, they're not going to believe we're just hanging out here forever."

Lilly suggested, "We need something that sounds believable but also gives us more time to figure this out."

Levi thought for a moment, then his eyes lit up with an idea. "How about this? We tell our parents that we're going to stay at Kellie's house for a week. We can say it's to support her father and make him feel less lonely. Plus, we can say we're bored without school and need a change of scenery."

Brittany nodded. "That could work. Kellie's dad might even appreciate the company and support."

Andrew agreed. "It's a solid plan. And it gives us the freedom to continue our investigation without raising suspicion."

Freddy added, "We just need to make sure our parents buy the story. We should all call them and explain it together."

Levi stood up, feeling more confident. "Alright, let's do this. We'll tell our parents we're planning to go to Kellie's house for at least a week. Let's make the calls now."

The group split up to call their parents, each of them using their most convincing tone. They explained how they wanted to support Kellie's father during this difficult time and how they thought it would be a good idea to spend a week at Kellie's house.

After several minutes of heartfelt conversations and a few reassuring words, the parents agreed. They believed the story and supported the idea, thinking it would be good for both the kids and Mr. Daniel.

Levi gathered everyone back in the living room. "We did it. Our parents are on board."

Andrew smiled. "Great job, everyone. Now we have a week to figure this out and find Kellie."

Brittany added, "Let's use this time wisely. We have a lot of work to do."

The team felt a renewed sense of purpose. They knew the risks were high, but their determination to find Kellie and uncover the truth kept them focused. With their parents' approval and a new plan in place, they were ready for the next phase of their daring mission.

Preparing for the Mission

Levi and Andrew met early the next morning, the excitement and nerves evident in their expressions. They had a mission to accomplish, and they were determined to succeed.

Levi looked at Andrew, his voice steady. "Are you ready for this?"

Andrew nodded, adjusting his backpack. "Absolutely. Let's do this."

They made their way to the local outdoor store, carefully selecting the items they would need for their journey into the unknown. Their shopping list included:

- **Backpacks:** To carry all necessary items.
- **Flashlights and Batteries:** Essential for navigating dark tunnels.
- **Rope:** For climbing or securing anything if needed.
- **Walkie-Talkies:** For communication if they get separated.
- **First Aid Kit:** For any injuries or emergencies.
- **Water and Snacks:** To stay hydrated and maintain energy levels.
- **Notebook and Pens:** To document any findings or map the tunnels.
- **Gloves:** To protect hands from rough surfaces or any hazardous materials.
- **Masks:** In case the air quality in the tunnel is poor.
- **Camera/Phone:** To take pictures of anything important.
- **Protective Clothing:** Sturdy shoes, jackets, and hats for protection.

They loaded up their backpacks with the gear, checking each item off their list to make sure they were prepared for anything.

That evening, Levi and Andrew headed to the supermarket. The plan was simple: observe and gather as much information as possible without drawing attention to themselves.

As they entered the store, they casually browsed the aisles, keeping an eye out for anything unusual. They made a few small purchases to blend in, but their real focus was on the employee-only areas.

Around 6 PM, they noticed something strange. From the employee-only access rooms, a group of people emerged. These individuals looked out of place—older, worn, and strangely dressed. They didn't look like the usual supermarket employees.

Levi nudged Andrew, whispering, "Look at them. They don't look like they work here."

Andrew nodded, his eyes narrowing. "Yeah, something's off. We need to keep watching."

The two boys continued to observe discreetly. They noticed that these strange individuals seemed to avoid interacting with the regular staff and quickly left the store, heading towards the back exit.

Levi's heart raced. "I bet they're coming from that underground lab."

After the strange group left, Levi and Andrew decided to follow them at a safe distance. They trailed the group through the back exit of the supermarket and saw them disappear into a small, nondescript building behind the store.

Andrew pulled out his notebook, jotting down the details. "This is it. This building must be the entrance to the tunnel."

Levi nodded, feeling a mix of excitement and fear. "We need to tell the others. We've found the way in."

They quickly returned to the supermarket, deciding not to make any more purchases to avoid raising suspicion. As they left the store, they discussed their next steps.

Andrew looked at Levi. "We'll need the whole team for this. It's too dangerous to go in alone."

Levi agreed. "Yeah, and we need to make sure we have all our gear ready. This isn't going to be easy."

As they walked back to Levi's house, they couldn't shake the feeling of anticipation. They had found the entrance to the mysterious underground facility, and now they needed to prepare for the journey that lay ahead.

Sharing the Discovery

Levi and Andrew hurried back to Levi's house, their minds racing with the excitement and danger of what they had discovered. As they entered the house, their friends looked up, eager for news.

"We found it," Andrew said, his voice breathless with excitement. "There's an entrance to the underground facility behind the supermarket."

Levi nodded. "Yeah, we saw a group of strange-looking people coming out of the employee-only access rooms. They don't look like they belong in a supermarket. We followed them, and they led us to a small building behind the store. That's got to be the entrance."

Ramy, always ready with a quip, grinned. "So, we're going to sneak into a spooky underground lab through the supermarket bathroom. This sounds like the plot of a really bad horror movie."

Freddy chuckled despite himself. "Yeah, except in those movies, everyone always dies."

Brittany rolled her eyes but smiled. "Let's hope our story has a better ending."

Lilly, trying to focus everyone, said, "Okay, so we know where the entrance is. What's the plan?"

Levi replied, "We need to get in when there are as few people as possible. It seems like most of the lab workers leave around 6 PM, so we should go in after that. There will probably still be a few guards, but it should be easier to handle."

Andrew added, "We need to be smart about this. We can't just walk in all at once. We'll go to the supermarket separately and meet in the bathrooms. Once everyone is there, we'll move to the employee-only access room and find the tunnel entrance."

Preparing for the Mission

The group nodded, feeling a mix of nerves and excitement. Ramy, trying to lighten the mood, said, "So, we're all going to the supermarket to hang out in the bathroom together. Sounds like a great Friday night."

Levi smirked. "Yeah, Ramy, maybe we'll start a new trend."

Freddy added, "I'll bring some air freshener. Those supermarket bathrooms can be pretty nasty."

The group couldn't help but laugh, the dark humor helping to ease their tension. They quickly packed their gear, making sure they had everything they needed: flashlights, walkie-talkies, ropes, and other essentials.

Levi checked his backpack one last time. "Alright, is everyone ready?"

Brittany nodded. "Let's do this."

They left Levi's house, telling their parents they were going to stay at Kellie's house to support her father. Once they had the necessary approvals, they made their way to the supermarket, arriving separately to avoid suspicion.

Levi went in first, heading straight to the bathroom. He checked the stalls, making sure they were empty.

Then, one by one, the rest of the group entered the supermarket and made their way to the bathroom. Once they were all there, Levi whispered, "Okay, let's wait here until the store closes. Then we'll move."

The minutes ticked by slowly, the group trying to stay as quiet as possible. Ramy, unable to resist, whispered, "I feel like we're in a really weird episode of 'Mission Impossible.' Next thing you know, Tom Cruise will be swinging from the ceiling."

Lilly giggled softly. "Shh, Ramy. We need to stay focused."

Finding the Tunnel Entrance

Finally, the store began to close, and the sounds of employees locking up filled the air. Levi peeked out of the bathroom, signaling to the group that it was time to move.

They crept out of the bathroom and made their way to the employee-only access room. Levi held his breath as he turned the doorknob, relieved to find it unlocked. They slipped inside, shutting the door quietly behind them.

Andrew pulled out his flashlight, illuminating the room. They scanned the area, and Levi spotted a hatch in the floor. "There it is," he whispered. "The entrance to the tunnel."

Freddy moved to help him lift the hatch, revealing a dark tunnel leading down. "This is it, guys. No turning back now."

Ramy, trying to keep the mood light, said, "Well, at least we didn't have to crawl through any vents. I've seen enough movies to know that never ends well."

They carefully climbed down the ladder into the tunnel, their flashlights cutting through the darkness. The air was cool and damp, and the tunnel seemed to stretch on forever.

Brittany took a deep breath. "Alright, let's go find Kellie."

With renewed determination, they began their journey through the tunnel, ready to uncover the secrets of the underground lab.

Lilly and Freddy, feeling the weight of the unknown, took a moment to pray. "Please, let Emily and Kellie be safe," Lilly whispered, her voice trembling. Freddy nodded, gripping her hand. "We need our sisters to be okay. Protect them, wherever they are." Their heartfelt prayers echoed softly in the dim tunnel.

9
Battle Beneath the Surface

As they moved deeper into the tunnel, the atmosphere grew more tense. Ramy, sensing the need to lighten the mood, couldn't resist a joke.

"You know," Ramy said, shining his flashlight ahead, "this feels like one of those horror movies where the audience is yelling at the screen, 'Don't go in there!' And here we are, going right in."

Andrew smirked. "Yeah, but we don't have much of a choice, do we?"

Ramy grinned. "Well, if we see any creepy clowns or weird dolls, I'm out of here."

Levi chuckled, feeling a bit of the tension ease. "Good to know where you draw the line, Ramy."

The tunnel seemed to stretch on forever, the damp air and echoing sounds adding to the eerie atmosphere. As they walked, they noticed strange markings on the walls, remnants of what appeared to be old construction signs.

Ramy, the comedian, pointed to one of the signs. "Look, 'Construction Zone: Enter at Your Own Risk.' Pretty sure they weren't talking about us."

Freddy laughed softly. "Yeah, but it feels like they were."

Brittany shivered. "Let's just keep moving. The sooner we find something, the better."

As they continued, they stumbled upon an old, rusted cart filled with random tools and debris. Ramy picked up a rusty wrench and held it up. "In case we run into any zombies, I've got this covered."

Lilly rolled her eyes but smiled. "You and your zombie apocalypse joke, Ramy."

Approaching the Lab Entrance

Finally, they reached a heavy metal door marked with faded letters that read "Authorized Personnel Only." Levi carefully pushed it open, revealing a dimly lit corridor.

"Well, here we go," Levi whispered.

Ramy added, "Remember, if we see any mad scientists, just act natural. Like, 'Oh, hey, we're here for the tour.'"

Andrew snorted. "Yeah, I'm sure that'll work."

As they stepped into the corridor, the reality of their mission hit them. They were about to uncover the secrets of the underground lab and, hopefully, find Kellie and the other missing children.

The corridor led to a series of rooms, each more mysterious than the last. The group moved cautiously, their flashlights illuminating old machinery and stacks of forgotten paperwork.

Ramy, trying to keep the mood light, said, "If we find any secret experiments, I call dibs on the superpowers."

Levi shook his head, amused. "Yeah, because that's exactly how it works, Ramy."

Brittany laughed quietly. "At least we'll have something to laugh about if we get out of here."

As they turned a corner, they found a room that seemed to be a control center. Screens lined the walls, and a large board displayed detailed information.

They carefully entered the room, their eyes scanning the walls covered with documents and diagrams. In the center of the room stood a large board, covered with photographs and notes.

Lilly approached the board, her flashlight illuminating its contents. "Guys, look at this."

The board displayed pictures of various lab scientists, complete with names and roles. Next to them were details about the number of guards and their assigned positions throughout the facility.

Andrew leaned in closer, reading one of the notes aloud. "Dr. Jenkins - Lead Scientist. Guards: 3 stationed at the main lab, 2 at the entrance, 4 on rotating patrol."

Levi, his eyes wide, said, "This is exactly what we need. We can figure out where everyone is."

Lilly quickly took out her camera and started snapping photos of the board. "We need to document everything. If we're going to navigate this place, we need all the information we can get."

Freddy nodded in agreement. "Good thinking, Lilly. We can use these photos to plan our movements."

Ramy, peeking over Lilly's shoulder, added, "I guess we know who to avoid now. And maybe who to bribe if we get caught."

Lilly continued to take photos of every strange and important thing they found, making sure they had a record of everything. "We can't miss anything. Every detail could be crucial."

Brittany pointed to a section of the board. "Look here. There's a map showing guard rotations and shift changes."

Andrew quickly took note. "Perfect. We can use this to avoid them. We need to move during a shift change to minimize the risk."

Levi felt a surge of hope. "This is our chance. If we're careful, we can get through this without being caught."

The team moved with renewed determination; their goal clear. They were one step closer to finding Kellie and uncovering the secrets hidden beneath their school.

The corridor led to a series of rooms, each more mysterious than the last. The group moved cautiously, their flashlights illuminating old machinery and stacks of forgotten paperwork.

Ramy, trying to keep the mood light, said, "If we find any secret experiments, I call dibs on the superpowers."

Levi shook his head, amused. "Yeah, because that's exactly how it works, Ramy."

Brittany laughed quietly. "At least we'll have something to laugh about if we get out of here."

As they turned a corner, they found a room that seemed to be a control center. Screens lined the walls, and a large map of the underground facility was pinned to a board.

Lilly pointed to the map. "Look, this shows the whole layout. There's the tunnel we came through, and there's another exit that leads to the supermarket."

Andrew examined the map closely. "We're in the right place. Now we just need to find the cells or rooms where they're keeping everyone."

Ramy glanced around. "Okay, let's move quickly. I don't want to stick around long enough to become a science experiment."

The team moved with renewed determination; their goal clear. They were one step closer to finding Kellie and uncovering the secrets hidden beneath their school.

Splitting Into Two Groups

The team stood in a dimly lit corridor; the tension palpable. Levi knew they had to cover more ground quickly and efficiently. He looked at his friends, determination in his eyes.

"Alright, we need to split up," Levi said, his voice steady. "Andrew, Lilly, you're with me. Ramy, Freddy, Brittany, you form the second group."

Ramy nodded, a rare moment of seriousness on his face. "Got it. We'll cover as much as we can."

Levi handed out walkie-talkies to everyone. "Stay in touch, and be safe. Take notes and photos wherever possible. We've got 10 guards down here, so let's stick to the plan."

They gathered around the map they had found in the control room, reviewing their strategy one last time.

"Here's the plan," Levi continued. "We've identified the control room where one guard is stationed. I've got some tablets for diarrhea," he said, holding up a small bottle. "We'll mix them into his coffee, and once he's out of commission, we'll tie him up in the bathroom."

Andrew smirked. "A bit unconventional, but it should work."

"Once he's out of the way, we'll use the surveillance equipment in the control room to identify the locations of all the guards,"

Levi explained. "We'll split up and take them out one by one, either tying them up or shutting them off somehow. This will give us a few hours to search for the kids."

Reaching the Control Room

Levi, Andrew, and Lilly made their way toward the control room, moving silently through the dimly lit corridors. They could see the glow of a computer screen from under the door, indicating that the guard was inside.

Andrew peered through a small window in the door. "He's sitting at the desk, drinking coffee. Perfect timing."

Levi carefully pulled out the bottle of tablets. "Alright, I'll make a strange noise to lure him out. Andrew, you mix these into his coffee when he comes to check."

Lilly nodded, her heart pounding. "Be careful, Levi."

Levi took a deep breath and found a spot nearby to create a distraction. He knocked over a metal bucket, making a loud clanging noise.

The guard inside the control room looked up, annoyed. "What the...?" He got up from his desk and opened the door to investigate the noise.

As soon as the guard stepped out into the corridor, Andrew slipped into the control room. He quickly poured the tablets into the guard's coffee, stirring it just enough to dissolve them. He then slipped back out, hiding behind a stack of crates.

The guard, not finding anything unusual, grumbled and went back into the control room. He took a sip of his coffee, completely unaware of what had just happened.

Levi, Andrew, and Lilly waited a few moments, their hearts racing. Soon, they heard the guard groaning, clutching his stomach.

"Damn, I think I'm sick," the guard muttered, rushing to the bathroom.

Levi, Andrew, and Lilly followed quietly. Once the guard was inside, they quickly tied him up and left him there, locking the door from the outside.

Back in the control room, Levi, Andrew, and Lilly pored over the surveillance screens, their hearts pounding with anticipation. The screens displayed various parts of the underground facility, revealing rooms and corridors they hadn't yet explored.

Levi scanned the screens quickly. "Look, there's a room full of beds. It looks like some sort of dormitory."

Andrew pointed to another screen. "And there, that looks like a common area. There are kids there!"

Lilly's eyes widened as she focused on one of the screens. "Oh my God, look! It's Kellie!"

They watched as Kellie and other children moved around the room, seemingly unaware of the cameras watching them. Tears of relief and joy welled up in their eyes.

Levi whispered, "We found them. We really found them."

Andrew nodded, unable to tear his eyes away from the screen. "They're all here. We did it."

Suddenly, Lilly gasped, pointing to another screen. "Look! It's Emily! My sister is there too!"

The emotions were overwhelming. They felt a rush of excitement and tears of happiness filled their eyes as they saw their loved ones safe, even if still trapped.

Freddy, Ramy, and Brittany joined them in the control room, and they all huddled around the screens, sharing the moment of discovery.

Ramy, trying to hold back his own tears, said, "Well, we found them. Now let's go get them out of there."

Freddy nodded; his voice choked with emotion. "Yeah, let's bring them home."

Levi took a deep breath, wiping his tears. "Alright, everyone. We know where they are. Let's get them out of here."

With renewed determination and a sense of urgency, the team prepared to move out, ready to rescue Kellie, Emily, and the other children from their captivity.

The team gathered around Levi in the control room, their faces a mix of relief and determination. Levi took a deep breath, knowing that the next steps were crucial.

"Alright, everyone," Levi began, "I'm going to stay here in the control room and guide you. I'll keep an eye on the screens and give you commands on what to do next. It's important that we stick to the plan and stay in communication at all times."

Andrew nodded, understanding the importance of having someone oversee the operation. "Sounds good, Levi. We'll follow your lead."

Lilly, still emotional from seeing her sister on the screen, added, "We trust you, Levi. Just tell us what to do."

Ramy, ever the joker, gave a mock salute. "Yes, Captain Levi! Ready for duty."

Freddy and Brittany shared a determined look, both agreeing silently.

Levi smiled at his friends' trust and confidence. "Okay, let's move out. Remember to keep your walkie-talkies on and follow my instructions. We need to do this quickly and quietly."

Andrew, Ramy, Freddy, Brittany, and Lilly each grabbed their gear and prepared to head out, knowing that they were now on a mission to save their friends and family.

Levi watched them leave, his heart pounding with a mix of fear and hope. He turned his attention back to the screens, ready to guide his friends through the final steps of their daring rescue mission.

Levi sat in the control room; his eyes glued to the surveillance screens. He picked up the walkie-talkie, his voice steady but urgent. "Andrew, Lilly, can you hear me?"

Andrew's voice crackled back. "Loud and clear, Levi."

Lilly added, "We're ready. What's the plan?"

Levi took a deep breath, scanning the screens. "Alright, listen carefully. There are two guards on the first floor near the children's lockup room. You need to move up there and take them out quietly. I'll guide you step by step."

Andrew replied, "Got it. Moving to the first floor now."

Levi watched as the camera showed Andrew and Lilly making their way up the stairs. "Okay, the first guard is patrolling the hallway. He's currently heading towards the far end. You have a few seconds to move."

Andrew whispered into the walkie-talkie, "We're on it."

They reached the top of the stairs and peeked around the corner. Levi's voice came through the walkie-talkie. "The guard just turned the corner. Move now, and hide behind the storage boxes on your left."

Andrew and Lilly moved quickly, ducking behind the boxes. They watched as the guard walked past, oblivious to their presence.

Levi continued, "Good. Now, wait for my signal. The second guard is coming from the opposite direction. He'll pass by in ten seconds. When he does, take him down quietly."

Lilly's heart pounded as she readied herself. "Understood."

They saw the second guard approaching. Levi counted down, "Three... two... one... now!"

Andrew and Lilly sprang into action. Andrew grabbed the guard from behind, covering his mouth and pulling him into a chokehold. Lilly quickly tied his hands and feet, securing him with rope.

Levi's voice came through again. "Great job. Now, move to the door on your right. The first guard will be back any second."

As they moved, the first guard reappeared, looking around suspiciously. Levi's voice was urgent. "He's coming your way. Hide behind the crates on your left."

Andrew and Lilly ducked behind the crates just in time. The guard walked past them, muttering to himself. Levi guided them step by step, his instructions precise.

"Wait for him to turn his back," Levi said. "Now, go!"

Andrew and Lilly moved swiftly, grabbing the guard and pulling him into a nearby room. They quickly subdued him, tying him up next to the other guard.

Levi's voice came through, filled with relief. "You did it. Both guards are secured. You're clear to move to the children's lockup room."

Andrew whispered, "Thanks, Levi. We couldn't have done it without you."

Lilly added, "We're heading to the lockup room now."

Levi watched them on the screen, his heart racing. They were getting closer to rescuing the children, but the challenges were far from over.

Andrew and Lilly cautiously approached the door to the children's lockup room. The dim light flickered overhead, casting eerie shadows along the corridor. Andrew held up his hand, signaling Lilly to stop as he gently turned the handle and pushed the door open.

Inside, they saw a room filled with small beds and a group of children huddled together. Among them were Kellie and Emily. The sight of their friends brought a surge of relief and emotion.

"Kellie! Emily!" Lilly whispered, her voice trembling with joy and relief.

Kellie looked up, her eyes widening in shock and then filling with tears. "Lilly! Andrew! You're really here!"

Andrew and Lilly rushed over, kneeling beside their friends. Kellie threw her arms around them, holding them tight. "I can't believe you found us," she sobbed.

Emily, looking pale but hopeful, whispered, "I knew you'd come. I just knew it."

Andrew, fighting back tears, gently pulled back to look at Kellie. "We're here to get you out. We have a plan, but we need to move quickly."

Kellie wiped her tears, nodding resolutely. "What do we need to do?"

Lilly explained, "Levi is in the control room, guiding us. We've taken out most of the guards, but we need to be ready to move fast. Can you get the other children ready?"

Kellie glanced around at the other kids, who were watching the reunion with a mix of hope and fear. "Yes, I can do that."

Andrew added, "We need to stay quiet and stick together. We'll lead you through the tunnel we came in. Once we're outside, we'll head straight to safety."

Kellie squeezed his hand, determination in her eyes. "We'll be ready. Just tell us when."

Lilly gave her a reassuring smile. "Stay strong, Kellie. We're almost out of here."

Andrew pulled out his walkie-talkie. "Levi, we've found them. They're all here."

Levi's voice came through, filled with emotion. "That's great news. Is Kellie there?"

Andrew handed the walkie-talkie to Kellie. "Levi wants to talk to you."

Kellie took the walkie-talkie, her voice breaking as she spoke. "Levi, it's me. Thank you so much. You saved us."

Levi's voice was steady but filled with emotion. "Kellie, I'm so glad you're safe. We're going to get you all out of there. Just hang tight a little longer."

Tears streamed down Kellie's face. "You've done so much for us. I can't believe you all risked so much."

Levi replied, "We're a team, Kellie. We look out for each other. We'll be together soon, I promise."

Kellie nodded, even though Levi couldn't see her. "Thank you, Levi. You've always been there for me. I don't know what we'd do without you."

Levi's voice cracked slightly. "We're almost there, Kellie. Just a little longer. Stay strong for the others."

Kellie handed the walkie-talkie back to Andrew, her eyes filled with gratitude and determination. "Let's do this."

Andrew looked at her and nodded. "We're ready. Levi, guide us out of here."

With renewed determination, they began to prepare the children for their escape, knowing that every second counted.

Back in the control room, Levi adjusted the surveillance screens and picked up his walkie-talkie. "Ramy, can you hear me?"

Ramy's voice crackled back. "Loud and clear, Captain Levi. What's our next move?"

Levi smiled, grateful for Ramy's humor to lighten the tense situation. "Alright, there's another lockup room on the east side of the facility. There are two guards patrolling the corridor. One of them looks pretty strong, so be prepared."

Freddy's voice chimed in, determined. "Got it. We're ready."

Levi watched the screens carefully. "Okay, Ramy, Brittany, and Freddy, move to the east corridor. Ramy, take the lead. I'll guide you step by step."

The team moved quietly through the dimly lit hallways, their flashlights illuminating the path ahead. Ramy couldn't resist a quip. "You know, Levi, I was hoping our first big mission together wouldn't involve so many creepy hallways."

Levi chuckled softly. "Focus, Ramy. The first guard is coming up on your left."

Ramy peeked around the corner and saw the guard approaching. He turned back to Freddy. "Alright, muscle man, this one's all you."

Freddy nodded, readying his rope. As the guard passed, Freddy jumped out and tackled him, quickly wrapping the rope around his wrists and ankles. The guard struggled, but Freddy's strength and determination held firm.

Levi's voice came through the walkie-talkie. "Good job, Freddy. Now move to the next position. There's another guard by the lockup room door."

Brittany, keeping an eye on their surroundings, added, "We need to move fast. He might notice the other guard is missing."

Levi guided them to the next corner. "Ramy, the second guard is ahead. He's standing right by the door. Be ready."

Ramy grinned. "Time to put on my best ninja impression."

As they approached the guard, Ramy and Brittany prepared to distract him. Ramy tossed a small rock down the hall, creating a noise that drew the guard's attention.

"What was that?" the guard muttered, stepping away from the door.

Freddy and Brittany seized the moment. Brittany used a flashlight to blind the guard momentarily, while Freddy tackled him from behind. They quickly tied him up with the rope, using duct tape to secure his mouth.

Ramy, adding a touch of dark humor, whispered, "You know, this reminds me of that time we tried to sneak into the movies. Except this time, it's a bit more serious."

Levi's voice came through, a mix of relief and urgency. "Great work, team. The lockup room is clear. Get the kids and move to the rendezvous point."

Ramy nodded, looking at Freddy and Brittany. "Alright, let's get those kids out of here."

They opened the door to the lockup room, finding more frightened children huddled together. Brittany reassured them, "We're here to help. We're getting you out of here."

Freddy added, "Stay close and stay quiet. We're going to keep you safe."

As they led the children out of the room, Ramy couldn't resist one last comment. "I've got to say, Levi, if we ever make it out of this, I'm writing a book about our adventures. Maybe call it 'How to Rescue Kids and Look Cool Doing It.'"

Levi laughed softly through the walkie-talkie. "Just get them out safely, Ramy. We can worry about the book later."

With Levi's guidance and the team's determination, they began to make their way to the rendezvous point, knowing that every step brought them closer to safety.

The Great Escape

Levi sat in the control room, watching the screens as the children were led out of their rooms. He picked up the walkie-talkie, his voice urgent but calm. "Andrew, Ramy, listen up. Get all the children to the tunnel entrance. We're meeting there. Move quickly and stay alert."

Andrew's voice crackled back. "Got it, Levi. We're on our way."

Ramy added, "Roger that. We'll get them there safely."

Levi took a deep breath, watching the screens as his friends moved cautiously through the corridors. "Lilly, make sure you keep the camera safe. We'll need it as evidence for the police."

Lilly replied, "Understood, Levi. I've got it secured."

As Andrew and Ramy's teams guided the children through the labyrinth of corridors, one of the tied-up guards managed to escape. He stumbled to an emergency button on the wall and slammed his fist against it.

The alarm blared through the facility, red lights flashing ominously. In the main control room, the remaining guards sprang into action, rushing to their positions. A voice echoed through the speakers, sending chills down everyone's spines. "Intruders in the lab! Secure all exits immediately!"

Levi's heart pounded as he heard the alarm. He picked up the walkie-talkie, his voice shaking. "Andrew, Ramy, get the kids to the tunnel now! Go, go, go!"

Andrew and Ramy's teams broke into a sprint, herding the children toward the tunnel entrance. Fear and panic gripped everyone, the urgency palpable. Children cried out, their faces pale with fear, while the older kids tried to help keep everyone calm.

Freddy led the way, his strong presence providing some reassurance to the frightened children. Brittany and Ramy brought up the rear, constantly glancing over their shoulders for any sign of the pursuing guards. The sounds of footsteps and shouts grew louder, adding to the tension.

Levi prepared to leave the control room, but just as he turned, the bathroom door burst open. The guard he had tied up earlier stood there, fury in his eyes. He lunged at Levi, slapping him hard across the face.

"Thought you could outsmart us, huh?" the guard snarled, his voice dripping with malice. He mocked Levi's leg, kicking it hard and causing Levi to stumble in pain. "What's the matter, can't run?"

The guard snatched the walkie-talkie from Levi's hand and threw it across the room, smashing it against the wall. "You're not going anywhere."

Levi, disoriented and in pain, tried to get up. "You won't get away with this," he spat, his voice defiant despite his fear.

The guard laughed cruelly. "We'll see about that."

The guard grabbed Levi by the collar and dragged him toward the control panel, mocking him with each step. "You thought you could just waltz in here and save the day? Pathetic."

Levi struggled, trying to break free, but the guard's grip was too strong. The pain in his leg was excruciating, making it difficult to fight back. The guard shoved him into a chair, tying him up with rough, biting ropes. "Stay put, hero."

Andrew and Ramy's teams, with the children in tow, reached the tunnel entrance. The alarm and flashing lights added to the chaos and fear. Brittany's voice quivered as she spoke, "We can't wait for Levi. We have to go now."

Tears streamed down Kellie's face. "We can't leave without him! We can't!"

Andrew, fighting back his own tears, grabbed Kellie's shoulders. "Kellie, we don't have a choice. If we stay, they'll catch us all. We have to keep the kids safe."

Kellie sobbed, resisting. "But Levi..."

Freddy, trying to hold back his emotions, urged the group forward. "We have to go. For Levi's sake, we have to protect the children."

As they reached the tunnel entrance, the sound of approaching guards grew louder. The new guards, alerted by the alarm, were closing in fast. The children, sensing the danger, began to cry and cling to their rescuers.

Andrew's voice was firm but filled with anguish. "We have to move now. We'll come back for Levi; I promise."

The group plunged into the tunnel, the children's sobs echoing in the darkness. The weight of leaving Levi behind was crushing, but they knew they had no other choice. They had to protect the children and escape to safety.

As they ran through the tunnel, the air filled with the sounds of their hurried footsteps and panicked breaths. Brittany carried a younger child who had tripped, whispering words of comfort despite her own fear.

Kellie's cries of anguish filled the tunnel as Andrew pulled her along. "We'll come back for him, Kellie. We'll come back."

The group pushed forward, driven by a mix of fear and determination. Their hearts were heavy with sorrow, but they knew they had to keep going. For Levi, for the children, and for the promise of freedom.

In the main control room, the lead security officer, Johnson, received an urgent call on his private line. The voice on the other end was cold and authoritative, filled with an eerie calmness.

"Johnson, this is Dr. Greaves. The situation is out of control. We cannot let this facility fall into the wrong hands. You know what to do."

Johnson, his face pale, replied, "But sir, there are still children and intruders inside. We can't just—"

Dr. Greaves cut him off. "Press the button to destroy the lab. It's an order. We cannot risk exposure. You have ten minutes."

With a resigned sigh, Johnson pressed the button. A deafening silence fell over the facility as all alarms suddenly stopped. For a brief moment, an eerie calm enveloped the underground complex.

The Countdown Begins

Levi, tied up in the control room, noticed the sudden silence. His heart raced, knowing something terrible was about to happen. The guard standing over him smirked, a cruel glint in his eyes.

The alarms blared again, this time with a new, chilling announcement. "Warning: Facility set to self-destruct. Evacuate immediately. Ten minutes remaining."

The countdown began, the numbers flashing ominously on every screen. Levi's eyes widened in shock. The guard laughed cruelly, leaning in close. "Looks like your little rescue mission just turned into a death sentence. We're getting out of here. You, however, are staying put."

Levi struggled against his bonds, desperation setting in. "You can't do this! There are innocent children here!"

The guard sneered. "Orders are orders. Enjoy the last few minutes of your life."

Andrew, Ramy, Freddy, Brittany, Kellie, Lilly, Ramy, Emily and the children were still running through the tunnel when the new announcement echoed around them. The words "self-destruct" and "ten minutes" sent waves of panic through the group.

Kellie, hearing the announcement, abruptly stopped running. She pulled her hand from Andrew's grasp, her eyes wide with fear and determination. "I can't move forward now. Let me go back and save Levi. He risked everything to save us. I can't leave him to die."

Andrew's heart broke at her words. "Kellie, we don't have time. If you go back, you might not make it out."

Kellie's voice shook with emotion. "I'd rather die trying to save him than live knowing I left him behind. Please, let me go."

Everyone stopped, torn between the urgency of escaping and the desperation to save their friend. Brittany and Ramy exchanged helpless looks, knowing there was little they could do to change her mind.

Freddy, his voice cracking, said, "Kellie, we understand. But be quick. We'll be waiting for you."

Kellie nodded, tears streaming down her face. She turned and ran back toward the facility, her heart pounding with every step.

The sound of the countdown echoed in her ears, a constant reminder of the limited time she had left.

Andrew watched her go, his own tears falling freely. "Be safe, Kellie."

With heavy hearts and tears in their eyes, the rest of the group continued toward the tunnel exit, knowing that their fight was far from over and praying that Kellie would make it back in time.

Final Minutes

As Kellie ran back towards the facility, determined to save Levi, Andrew's voice rang out, filled with urgency and emotion. "Kellie, stop!"

Kellie turned, tears streaming down her face. "I have to go, Andrew. I can't leave him behind."

Andrew ran to her, his own eyes filled with tears. "You're not going alone. Let me join you. I don't want to live my life with the guilt of not trying to save him."

Ramy stepped forward, for the first time showing a deep emotional side. "I'm coming too. Kellie and Levi have always been there for me. I can't let them face this alone."

Freddy, his voice trembling, added, "We're all in this together. We can't leave anyone behind."

Brittany, close to Andrew, said, "I'm coming too. We can't let them do this alone."

Lilly, clutching the camera tightly, nodded. "We're a team. We started this together, and we'll finish it together."

Andrew, his voice strong but filled with emotion, spoke up. "No, there should be someone to protect the children. Brittany, Freddy, and Lilly, you stay back and safeguard the kids. If we don't make it, you need to expose this to the world."

Ramy, his voice cracking, added, "Please. If we don't come back, you need to make sure everyone knows what happened here."

Brittany, tears streaming down her face, hugged Andrew tightly. "Promise me you'll come back."

Freddy nodded; his eyes filled with determination. "We will. Just make sure the kids are safe."

Lilly, holding back her sobs, agreed. "We'll get them to safety and make sure everyone knows what you all did."

With heavy hearts and tears in their eyes, Brittany, Freddy, and Lilly turned back to lead the children to safety, their steps filled with the weight of their friends' sacrifice.

Andrew, Ramy, and Kellie, knowing the risks but driven by love and loyalty, ran back toward the facility, determined to save Levi. The speaker blared, announcing that only four minutes remained until the lab would be destroyed.

An Emotional Goodbye

Andrew, Ramy, and Kellie rushed back toward the facility, determined to save Levi. Their hearts pounded with fear and determination as they sprinted through the dimly lit corridors, the countdown blaring in their ears.

Meanwhile, Lilly, Brittany, and Freddy led the children towards the end of the tunnel. The cool night air beckoned them, promising safety and freedom. The children, sensing the urgency, moved as quickly as their small legs could carry them.

Lilly clutched the camera tightly, her mind racing. "We need to get these kids out. We need to expose this."

Freddy nodded; his eyes filled with worry. "They'll make it. Andrew, Kellie, and Ramy will get Levi. We have to believe that."

Brittany, tears streaming down her face, tried to comfort the children. "It's okay, we're almost there. Just a little further."

The end of the tunnel was in sight, the light from the exit casting a glow that seemed to promise safety. But just as they were about to step out, the speaker crackled to life, the voice cold and final. "Warning: Facility self-destruct in 10 seconds. 10... 9... 8..."

Lilly's heart sank, and she turned to look back into the tunnel. "No... they have to make it."

Freddy grabbed her hand, pulling her towards the exit. "We have to go. Now!"

As they emerged from the tunnel into the open air, the countdown reached its final seconds. "3... 2... 1..."

A deafening explosion rocked the ground beneath them, and a massive cloud of smoke and debris erupted from the tunnel entrance. The force of the blast knocked them to the ground, and for a moment, the world seemed to stand still.

The group scrambled to their feet, their ears ringing and hearts pounding. They turned to look back at the tunnel, now partially collapsed and filled with smoke and rubble. The realization hit them all at once—Andrew, Ramy, Kellie, and Levi were still inside.

Brittany fell to her knees, sobbing uncontrollably. "No... they can't be gone. They can't be."

Freddy, tears streaming down his face, hugged her tightly. "We have to believe they made it out. We have to."

Lilly stood in shock, clutching the camera to her chest. "We promised we'd get out together. We promised."

The children, confused and frightened, began to cry, their small voices adding to the chorus of grief. Lilly, Brittany, and Freddy did their best to comfort them, but their own hearts were breaking.

They stood at the edge of the tunnel, staring back at the destruction, their minds filled with the images of their friends running back into danger. The weight of their loss settled heavily on their shoulders, and they couldn't hold back their tears.

Brittany whispered through her sobs, "They were heroes. They went back to save him."

Freddy nodded, his voice trembling. "We have to remember them. We have to make sure the world knows what they did."

Lilly, her face streaked with tears, held the camera up. "We will. We'll make sure everyone knows."

The group huddled together, their hearts heavy with sorrow, but filled with a fierce determination. They had escaped, but their mission was far from over. They would honor their friends' sacrifice by telling their story and making sure the world knew the truth about the horrors beneath the school swimming pool.

The Aftermath and Revelation

As Lilly, Brittany, Freddy, and the children stumbled out of the tunnel, they were met by a crowd of local people who had gathered, drawn by the sound of the explosion and the sight of smoke rising from the tunnel entrance. The community had come together, worried and curious about what had happened.

An elderly man from the crowd stepped forward, concern etched on his face. "Are you all alright? What happened?"

Lilly, still clutching the camera, nodded shakily. "We... we need help. There are children who need medical attention. Please, call the police and an ambulance."

The crowd sprang into action, some people using their phones to call emergency services, while others tried to comfort the children and offer them water and blankets. The sirens of police cars and ambulances soon filled the air, growing louder as they approached the scene.

Freddy's father, Officer Matthew, was among the first to arrive. He rushed over, his face a mixture of relief and fear. "Freddy! Thank God you're safe!" He pulled Freddy into a tight embrace, his voice choked with emotion. "I was so worried."

Freddy hugged him back, tears streaming down his face. "Dad, there's so much you need to know. We found the missing children... but we lost some friends in the process."

Officer Matthew pulled back, his eyes searching Freddy's. "Tell me everything."

Local reporters and paper media had also arrived, their cameras flashing and microphones thrust forward as they tried to capture the story. Lilly, Brittany, and Freddy began to explain what had happened, showing the camera and the footage they had recorded as evidence.

Lilly spoke to the reporters, her voice strong despite her tears. "We discovered a hidden facility under the school swimming pool. They were experimenting on children. We have the proof here. Please, help us make sure this never happens again."

As the police took the children and their rescuers to the hospital for treatment, Officer Matthew examined the footage and the evidence they had collected. His expression grew more serious with each passing moment.

"I should have believed you from the start," he said, his voice filled with regret. "I'm so sorry for doubting you. You've all shown incredible bravery."

Brittany's father, a local mechanic, joined them, his eyes filled with pride and sorrow. "You kids did something incredible today. We're all so proud of you."

The parents of Ramy, Levi, and Kellie arrived, their faces pale with worry. Mrs. Hassan, Ramy's mother, cried out, "Where's my son? Where's Ramy?"

Lilly stepped forward, her heart aching. "They... they went back to save Levi. We haven't seen them since the explosion."

Kellie's father, Mr. Daniel, looked stricken. "No... my daughter... she was so brave..."

The crowd tried their best to comfort the grieving parents, offering words of solace and support. The atmosphere was heavy with a mix of relief for the rescued children and sorrow for those who were still missing.

Freddy's father, struggling to keep his composure, addressed the crowd. "We will find them. We will do everything in our power to bring them back. These children have shown us what true courage looks like, and we owe it to them to never give up."

The reporters captured the emotional scene, broadcasting it to the world. The story of the brave children and their incredible rescue mission spread quickly, touching hearts and raising awareness about the hidden horrors beneath the school.

As the children were taken to the hospital for further treatment, the community came together, united by the bravery and sacrifice of their young heroes.

10
Remembering their friends

Remembering the Brave

Two days had passed since the dramatic rescue and the destruction of the hidden facility. Lilly, Freddy, and Brittany had been treated at the hospital and were now recovering.

They decided to meet at their usual spot, the old oak tree at the edge of the playground, a place filled with memories of their missing friends.

The sun was setting, casting long shadows across the ground as they gathered under the tree's wide branches. The air was heavy with the weight of their loss, and the usually comforting shade of the tree felt somber.

Lilly leaned against the tree trunk; her eyes red from crying. "I can't believe they're gone. Levi, Andrew, Ramy... They were so brave."

Freddy sat on one of the tree roots, staring at the ground. "Andrew always knew what to do. He was like a big brother to all of us. I keep expecting him to show up and tell us it was all a bad dream."

Brittany, hugging her knees to her chest, whispered, "Ramy was always the one who made us laugh, even in the darkest times. He had this way of making everything seem less scary."

Lilly nodded, her voice trembling. "And Levi... he was the heart of our group. Always thinking about everyone else, always putting others first. He saved us all."

They sat in silence for a moment, each lost in their memories. The pain of their absence was a physical ache, a void that seemed impossible to fill.

Freddy broke the silence, his voice cracking. "Do you remember that time Levi convinced us to build that treehouse? He wouldn't let us quit, even when it seemed impossible."

Brittany managed a small smile through her tears. "Yeah, and Ramy was the one who kept making jokes about how it was going to fall apart at any moment. But it didn't. It stood because Levi wouldn't let us give up."

Lilly wiped her eyes, the tears still flowing. "Andrew was the one who figured out how to make the ladder stable. He was always the problem solver."

The three friends continued to share memories, each story bringing a mixture of smiles and tears. The weight of their loss pressed down on them, making it hard to breathe.

Freddy looked around at their familiar meeting spot, now filled with an overwhelming sense of emptiness. "It doesn't feel right being here without them. This was our place, all of us together."

Brittany nodded, her voice barely a whisper. "I don't think I can stay here. Not without them."

Lilly hugged herself, trying to hold back the sobs that threatened to overtake her. "Maybe we need to find a new place. Somewhere we can remember them, but also move forward. They'd want us to keep going."

Freddy stood up, helping Brittany to her feet. "You're right. They'd want us to be strong. But it's so hard."

Lilly joined them, her heart heavy. "We'll find a way. Together."

As they walked away from the old oak tree,

A strange feeling of both sadness and peace settled over them. The memories of their missing friends weighed heavily on their hearts.

Just as they were about to leave the clearing, Brittany suddenly stopped, her eyes widening. "Did you hear that?" she whispered, her voice trembling.

Freddy turned to her, confused. "Hear what?"

Brittany's eyes filled with tears as she looked back at the tree. "I thought I heard Kellie's voice. She said, 'Don't leave us.'"

Lilly felt a chill run down her spine. "I heard it too. But it can't be..."

They exchanged a look of disbelief, and then, as if on cue, a soft voice floated through the air. "Guys, wait!"

Freddy's heart skipped a beat. "That sounded like Andrew!"

They stood frozen, torn between hope and the fear of their imaginations playing tricks on them. Then, a familiar, lighthearted voice echoed from behind the tree. "You didn't think you could get rid of us that easily, did you?"

Ramy's unmistakable humor brought tears to their eyes. Lilly turned to her friends, her voice shaking. "I heard it too. Ramy... he's here."

Freddy and Brittany nodded; their faces wet with tears. "We all heard it," Freddy said, his voice filled with a mix of hope and disbelief.

Suddenly, from behind the tree, Ramy stepped out with a big grin on his face, his eyes sparkling with mischief. "Miss us?"

Brittany let out a cry of joy and disbelief. "Levi! Ramy! Andrew! Kellie!"

Andrew and Kellie appeared next, looking exhausted but alive. The three friends who were presumed lost were standing right in front of them, safe and sound. The sight was almost too much to believe.

Lilly, Freddy, and Brittany ran towards them, tears of joy streaming down their faces. They collided in a group hug, holding each other tightly, their sobs of relief and happiness filling the air.

Kellie, tears streaming down her cheeks, whispered, "We made it. We couldn't leave you."

Andrew, his voice choked with emotion, said, "We promised we'd come back."

Ramy, ever the joker, added with a grin, "Did you really think a little explosion could stop us?"

As they hugged and cried, Freddy's father, Officer Matthew, approached, his face filled with pride and joy. "I knew you'd make it," he said, his voice thick with emotion.

Freddy looked up at his father, tears in his eyes. "Dad, they're alive. They made it."

Officer Matthew nodded, his own eyes glistening with tears. "Yes, they did. And you all did something incredible today."

The group stood together, holding each other, the weight of the past days' events lifting off their shoulders. The oak tree, which had seemed like a place of sadness, now felt like a place of miracles.

As the group stood together, tears of joy streaming down their faces, they couldn't stop hugging each other. The relief and happiness were almost overwhelming.

Lilly, still holding onto Kellie, Levi laughed through her tears. "I can't believe it. I thought we lost you forever."

Andrew smiled, his eyes twinkling. "It's going to take more than a collapsing tunnel to get rid of us."

Ramy, ever the comedian, added, "Yeah, and besides, who else would be here to make fun of Freddy's hair?"

Freddy chuckled, wiping his eyes. "I missed you too, Ramy. I missed your terrible jokes."

Brittany looked at Andrew, her voice full of emotion. "I'm so glad you're okay. I don't know what we would have done without you."

Andrew hugged her tightly. "We're back, and that's all that matters."

As they continued to share their joy, someone noticed Levi standing a bit apart, leaning on a crutch with a big bandage wrapped around his leg. Lilly rushed to him, her eyes wide with concern.

"Levi! What happened to your leg?" she exclaimed, tears of worry now mixing with her joy.

Levi gave a reassuring smile. "It's just a sprain. I'll be fine. The doctor said it looks worse than it is."

Ramy couldn't resist. "Yeah, Levi had to save the day while looking cool with a crutch. Typical hero stuff."

Levi laughed. "Yeah, sure, Ramy. But seriously, it's good to be back with all of you."

Andrew, noticing Levi's leg, said, "You're a true hero, Levi. You saved us all. We couldn't have done it without you."

Freddy, his eyes shining with pride, added, "Yeah, Levi, you're the reason we're all standing here together."

Lilly nodded; her voice filled with gratitude. "You're the heart of our team, Levi."

Levi, touched by their words, said, "We did this together. Every single one of us."

After the initial reunion, Freddy's curiosity got the better of him. "What happened after we left the lab? How did you manage to escape? We saw it destroyed right in front of our eyes."

Andrew, Ramy, and Kellie exchanged looks, their expressions turning serious as they prepared to recount their harrowing experience.

Andrew started, "Well, after you guys left, we made our way back to the control room. We had to think quickly."

Ramy, Andrew, and Kellie sprinted through the dimly lit corridors, their breaths coming in ragged gasps. The announcement blared through the speakers, "Facility self-destruct in 2 minutes."

Andrew glanced at Ramy; his voice strained. "We don't have much time. We have to reach Levi and get out of here."

Kellie nodded; her face determined despite the fear in her eyes. "We can't leave him behind."

They rounded a corner and entered a damaged funnel-like passageway, debris already starting to fall around them. The sight of the destruction was terrifying, and they knew there was no turning back.

"Stay close and keep moving!" Andrew shouted; his voice barely audibles over the noise.

As they reached the control room, they saw Levi struggling to stand, his leg beaten badly by the guard. Kellie rushed to him, tears streaming down her face. "Levi!"

Levi looked up; pain etched on his face. "Kellie... Andrew... Ramy... we need to get out of here."

The announcement echoed ominously, "Facility self-destruct in 1 minute."

Andrew and Ramy pulled Levi to his feet, supporting him between them. "We have to move, now!" Andrew urged.

With Levi leaning heavily on them, they started to make their way out. But as they reached the entrance of the tunnel, they saw it had collapsed, blocking their path.

Kellie looked at Levi, panic in her eyes. "The tunnel to the shop has completely collapsed. What do we do now?"

Levi, gritting his teeth against the pain, said, "I remember the map... There's another way out. It's in the control room. We need to find it."

Kellie nodded, determination filling her eyes. "I'll get it."

As the labs began to crumble around them, the power cut out, plunging them into darkness. They quickly switched on their flashlights, the beams cutting through the dust and debris.

Kellie hurried back into the control room, her heart pounding. The debris and falling equipment made it difficult to navigate, but she pushed forward, knowing they had no time to waste.

"40 seconds remaining," the announcement droned.

Frantically, Kellie searched through the wreckage, her flashlight flickering. She finally spotted the map, half-buried under a fallen monitor. She grabbed it and turned back, dodging falling debris and jumping over obstacles.

Outside, Andrew and Ramy were struggling to keep Levi moving, the countdown ticking away in their ears. "Come on, Kellie!" Ramy muttered, his grip tightening on Levi.

Kellie emerged from the control room, holding the map aloft. "I've got it! Let's go!"

They scanned the map quickly. Levi pointed to the third exit route. "There! That's our way out!"

Supporting Levi between them, they started running towards the third exit. The facility shook violently, debris falling around them as the countdown continued. "30 seconds remaining."

They navigated the narrow corridors, the ground trembling beneath their feet. The sounds of destruction grew louder, and the air was thick with dust and smoke.

"10 seconds remaining," the announcement blared, sending a fresh wave of panic through them.

Andrew and Ramy pushed themselves harder, half-carrying, half-dragging Levi. They could see the third exit ahead, a faint glimmer of hope in the chaos.

"5... 4... 3... 2..."

With a final burst of energy, they reached the exit, diving through just as the facility began to implode. They tumbled out into a dimly lit tunnel that continued to stretch far ahead. They hadn't reached the open air yet; they were in another tunnel that led to a different place.

Breathing heavily, covered in dust and debris, they clung to each other, knowing they had narrowly escaped death but still had a journey ahead of them. The realization hit them that their ordeal wasn't over yet. They had made it out of the immediate danger, but they still needed to find their way to safety.

Andrew, Ramy, Kellie, and Levi stumbled through the tunnel, the dim light barely illuminating their path. The air was thick with dust, and every step felt like a struggle. Finally, they saw a faint light ahead and emerged into a large basement room. They climbed the stairs cautiously, emerging into a grand hallway.

Andrew looked around, his eyes narrowing in suspicion. "Where are we?"

Kellie pointed to a framed photo on the wall, her voice trembling. "Look! It's Principal Nicholas. This is his house."

The group stared at the photo, a sense of disbelief washing over them. The opulence of the house stood in stark contrast to the chaos they had just escaped. The polished floors, ornate furniture, and elegant decor all seemed so out of place.

Ramy, his voice filled with shock, said, "Why would the principal's house be connected to the lab? This is insane."

Levi, leaning on Kellie for support, added, "We need to get out of here. If the principal is involved, we're not safe."

They moved through the house cautiously, their senses on high alert. The silence was eerie, and every creak of the floorboards made them jump. They searched for an exit, their urgency growing with each passing moment.

Finally, they found a back door and slipped out into the night. The cool air was a relief, but their hearts were still racing. They made their way through the backyard and out onto a quiet street.

After a tense journey, they reached the hospital. Exhausted and injured, they stumbled through the emergency entrance. The staff quickly took notice, rushing to help them.

As they were being treated, Levi managed to explain, "We need the police. There's a hidden facility under the school. We barely made it out."

The hospital staff alerted the authorities, and soon the police arrived, including Officer Matthew, Freddy's father.

After a tense journey, they reached the hospital. Exhausted and injured, they stumbled through the emergency entrance. The staff quickly took notice, rushing to help them.

As they were being treated, Levi managed to explain, "We need the police. There's a hidden facility under the school. We barely made it out."

The hospital staff alerted the authorities, and soon the police arrived. Officer Matthew, Freddy's father, was already at the other hospital with Lilly's team when he received the urgent call about Levi's group. His face turned serious as he listened to the message.

"Stay here," he told Lilly, Brittany, and the other children.

He rushed out of the hospital, his mind racing with worry, and arrived at the hospital where Levi's team was being treated.

Matthew rushed in, his face a mixture of worry and relief. He saw Levi, Andrew, Ramy, and Kellie, all battered but alive. "Are you all okay?"

Andrew, still shaken but safe, nodded. "It's not just about us. There's so much more. The principal's involved. We found his house connected to the lab."

Matthew's expression turned serious as he listened to their story. The bravery and determination of the kids were evident in their words and actions.

"Levi, Andrew, Ramy, Kellie, you all did something incredible," Matthew said, his voice filled with emotion. "I'm so sorry I didn't believe you earlier. You've shown more courage than most adults could."

Levi, his voice trembling, added, "We just wanted to save our friends."

Matthew hugged them tightly, tears streaming down his face. "I'm so proud of you. You all did something amazing. And thank you for saving Emily. You saved my daughter."

Kellie, her own eyes filling with tears, replied, "We couldn't leave anyone behind. We did it together."

Matthew nodded, his voice breaking. "You all risked your lives to save others. That's true bravery."

The police took statements from each of the children, and the hospital staff continued to treat their injuries. The relief of being safe was overwhelming, but the weight of what they had discovered and survived was still heavy on their minds.

As they sat together in the hospital, the reality of their ordeal began to sink in. They had uncovered a dark secret, faced incredible dangers, and come out on the other side stronger and more united than ever.

The Revelation

As Levi, Andrew, Ramy, and Kellie finished recounting their harrowing escape and the shocking discovery of the principal's house, Lilly, Brittany, and Freddy sat in stunned silence. The weight of the revelations hung heavily in the air.

Lilly was the first to speak, her voice barely above a whisper. "I can't believe Principal Nicholas is involved. It's like a nightmare."

Freddy, shaking his head in disbelief, added, "How could someone who's supposed to care for us be behind something so horrible?"

Brittany, her eyes wide with shock, asked, "But why? Why would he do this? What could he possibly gain from running a lab like that?"

Andrew, his face grim, replied, "We don't know for sure. But whatever it was, it must have been something big. People don't go to these lengths for nothing."

Kellie nodded; her voice filled with determination. "We need to find out. We can't let this go unanswered."

Ramy, his usual humor absent, said, "Yeah, we need to know why he did this. And we need to make sure he can't hurt anyone else."

Freddy's father, Officer Matthew, who had been listening intently, interjected, "The police are already looking into it. But your testimonies and the evidence you've gathered will be crucial in bringing him to justice."

Lilly, her mind racing, asked, "But what happened to Principal Nicholas? Where is he now?"

Brittany, echoing Lilly's question, added, "Why was he behind this mysterious lab? What was he trying to achieve?"

The room fell silent again, the unanswered questions hanging in the air. The mystery of Principal Nicholas's motives and whereabouts loomed over them, a dark shadow that needed to be brought into the light.

11
The Aftermath and the New Threat

The government swiftly shut down the school, closing off all access to the now-exposed underground facility. The scandal rocked the community, but out of the chaos, a new sense of hope emerged.

Officer Matthew, deeply moved by the bravery of Levi and his friends, helped them enroll in a new school. He generously covered Levi's fees, ensuring that the group could stay together and continue their education without interruption.

As the weeks passed, Levi, Andrew, Ramy, Kellie, Lilly, Brittany, and Freddy began to settle into their new school. The trauma of their ordeal slowly started to fade, replaced by the joy of newfound safety and friendship.

They walked to school each morning with a renewed sense of purpose, their bond stronger than ever. They knew they had faced something extraordinary together and had come out the other side, ready to take on whatever life threw at them next.

The Terrifying Call

One evening, Freddy, Lilly, Matthew, and his wife were sitting in the living room, discussing the recent events. The comfortable surroundings provided a stark contrast to the harrowing experiences they had endured.

Freddy's mother, her face filled with concern, asked, "How are you all holding up?"

Lilly smiled weakly. "We're getting there. It helps to talk about it and know we're not alone."

Matthew nodded in agreement. "You all did something remarkable. You saved lives."

Just then, the phone rang. Matthew reached over to answer it, switching it to speaker mode out of habit. "Hello, this is Matthew."

A chilling voice crackled through the line. "Good evening, Officer Matthew."

Matthew's blood ran cold. "Who is this?"

"This is Dr. Greaves," the voice continued, filled with malice. "I'm sure you've heard of me. I'm Principal Nicholas's brother."

Matthew's eyes widened in shock. Freddy and Lilly, sitting nearby, exchanged terrified looks but remained silent, listening intently.

Dr. Greaves's voice dripped with venom. "We created that lab to find a cure for my brother's daughter. She has a rare disease that no doctor could cure. We were close, so close, until your children destroyed everything."

Matthew clenched his fists. "You used innocent children as test subjects. That's monstrous."

Dr. Greaves laughed harshly. "Desperate times call for desperate measures. We spent huge amounts of time and money building that underground tunnel with three exits. One led to the shop, another directly to my brother Principal Nicholas's house, and the third through the swimming pool where we accessed and tested some children with injections for short-term experiments without their knowledge. But these kids ruined everything."

Matthew, his voice trembling with anger, said, "You have no right to put children at risk for your experiments. We'll make sure you pay for this."

Dr. Greaves's tone turned even more sinister. "You think you can stop us? We have many underground facilities like the one you destroyed. If you and your brave little kids think you can take us down, go ahead and try. But know this, Officer Matthew, I will not let this go. Those children will pay for what they've done."

In the background, they could hear Principal Nicholas crying out in despair and anger, cursing the fate that had befallen his daughter.

The call ended abruptly, leaving a deafening silence in its wake. Matthew, pale and shaken, turned to Freddy and Lilly, who were both visibly scared.

Freddy whispered, his voice trembling, "We're not safe. What are we going to do?"

Matthew hugged Freddy, Lilly, and Emily tightly, his mind racing. "We'll protect each other. We'll stay strong. But we have to be prepared. This isn't over."

The room felt colder, the once safe haven now filled with a sense of impending danger. They knew they were facing a new, more sinister threat. The fight for their safety and justice had only just begun.

--------------------End of Story Part — 1----------------------

Dear Reader,

Your journey through "Lost at the School Swimming Pool - Mystery of the Missing Kids" means the world to me. As an author, your engagement and feedback are invaluable.

I hope this story has sparked your imagination, tugged at your heartstrings, and provided a thrilling adventure.

Your thoughts and feedback are crucial in helping me improve and continue creating stories that captivate and inspire.

If you have a moment, I would be incredibly grateful if you could share your honest feedback on Amazon.

Your review can make a significant difference and helps other readers discover this story.

Steps to Leave Your Feedback:

1. Open your camera app.
2. Point your mobile device at the QR code below.
3. The review page will appear in your web browser.

or

visit http://www.amazon.com/review/create-review?&asin=9798334471917

Thank You

Stay tuned for the next thrilling instalment of "Lost at the School Swimming Pool - The Mystery of the Missing Kids," where new secrets will be unearthed, new allies will emerge, and the fight for justice will take on even more dangerous twists and turns.

Thanks
Hamza Ansari
hamzadotinfo@gmail.com

Made in the USA
Las Vegas, NV
15 December 2024